Everybody knows you can't take anything
with you when you die… lmost everybody.

Taking
It
With You

By Daniel Prokop

Also by this author:

I CAN EAT BOOGERS TOO
(Parenting Stories to Warm the Cockles of your Heart and
Wet the Tip of your Finger)

"A warm, laughter-filled collection of parenting stories that take the reader on a no-holds-barred journey through the everyday glories and agonies of parenting: From the grand to the ridiculous, from the heart-rending to the maddening, naked and true. Look in this mirror and you see a bit of all of us. And you feel a bit less alone, like it is all even more worthwhile." By Robin Grille: internationally acclaimed author of PARENTING FOR A PEACEFUL WORLD and HEART TO HEART PARENTING.

"An adorable account of parenthood and childhood. With delightful Aussy humor, I felt the heart of this book and enjoyed many giggles. This book reads like a string of pearls. I will be reading it again and again!" Amazon Review by Tahila Chante.

"This is a hoot! Even better, it is an honest, heartfelt hoot. Daniel has taken everyday challenges of parenting and child-raising and rendered them into funny and insightful stories that point the way to compassionate, honest, respectful parenting. The real joy of this book is its love." Amazon review by Owen

"A funny, gentle and honest read about being a parent, with lots of thoughtful reflections on life and love, that make you smile." Amazon review by Andrew

Available as e-book and paperback: ISBN: 978-0980828870
140 pages. Paperback H x W: 230mm x 150mm

Also by this author:

LEAVING NEVERLAND
(Why Little Boys Shouldn't Run Big Corporations)

"An insightful depiction of the dangers we face in having the perpetual 'boys' of this world in positions of power – incomplete men with arrested development. The style, pace, and delightful skewering are reminiscent of Hunter S Thomson!" ~ Rex Finch, Finch Publishing.

"An amusing read. I enjoyed the sustained concept of children (small male children, primarily) being allowed to run the nursery and getting it horribly wrong." ~J. S. Watts author of A DARKER MOON

"You really cracked me up - I couldn't stop laughing. My husband honestly thought I'd lost the plot... such an entertaining read." K. K. Jones.

Quotes from the book:
"Childhood is meant to be a life stage, not a lifestyle choice."

"In a desperate attempt to stay young forever we have achieved eternal childishness, rather than eternal youth."

"Behind every preventable threat to the future of the human race lurks a boy in a man's body with both of his hands buried deep in the cookie jar set aside for future generations."

Available as e-book and paperback: ISBN: 978-0-9808288-0-1
252 pages. Paperback H x W: 230mm x 150mm

www.danielprokop.com

Published by
Continuum Australia Pty Ltd
First published 2012

www.danielprokop.com

© 2012 Daniel Prokop
The moral right of the author has been asserted
National Library of Australia
Cataloging- in- Publication data

Prokop, Daniel
Taking It With You / Daniel Prokop
ISBN: 978-0-9808288-4-9
Dewey Number: A823.4

Inspirational Fiction, Humor, Buddhism, Reincarnation,
Tibet, Death, Dying

All the characters in this book are the product of the author's imagination and
any resemblance to actual people, living or dead, is entirely coincidental except
for Isabel Losada. Isabel did organize a 'Reward the Dalai Lama' stunt at Nelson's
Column which she writes about in her book "For Tibet with Love." Isabel has
kindly given me permission to use her and her inspired event in this novel.

Corporations or institutions mentioned herein are either imaginary or, if real,
used fictitiously without any intent to describe actual conduct. The Gyuto Monks
are the chant masters of Tibet, the Students for a Free Tibet, and the International
Campaign for Tibet are both amazing active international organizations and
permission has been granted for them to be included.

www.gyuto.co
www.studentsforafreetibet.org
www.savetibet.org

*"In our
struggle
for freedom,
truth is the only
weapon we possess."*

*~ His Holiness,
the 14th Dalai Lama*

"After all, it is no more surprising to be born twice, than it is to be born once." ~ Voltaire

Chapter 1

The sound of the clock steals into Faith McCormack's awareness, robbing focus from the numbers that cascade across an extensive bank of computer screens. Concentration broken, Faith promptly assumes the exhausted posture that she knows too well. Bracing her elbows on the polished mahogany of the desk she slumps forward. The palms of her hands support her head.

Without thinking she rubs her palms into her tired eyes. Suddenly she snaps upright. Bugger! Bugger! Bugger! She stares at the smudged make-up on her hands. The exorbitantly expensive cosmetics no longer conceal the unwelcome black bags that lurk below her green irises. Double bugger!

The damage done; she resumes her position. Faith takes a precious moment, to just stare into the nothingness behind her eyelids. The only sound is the clock...

TICK, TICK, TICK, TICK

... slow and steady, relentless. "Every tick is a tiny debit against one's lifespan, correction, my lifespan." God, how morbid. Where did that come from? Faith has no time for this kind of thinking and the full irony of that is not wasted. "When did I ever have time?" she wonders.

When Faith lifts her head, she sees the clock, her clock, her trophy. It was the *pièce de résistance* of an office that looked down on the glass ceiling. No other woman had reached the rarified heights that Faith McCormack had.

The clock is an exact replica of the clock that dominates the largest open outcry trading floor in the world. Just as the clock dominates the Chicago Mercantile Exchange, so Faith dominates commodity trading in currencies, oil, and of course her shiny favorite, gold.

The second hand moves brazenly towards the twelve, unaware of the chaos, semi-organized chaos, that it is about to unleash many floors below. The first chime sends Faith back 18 years earlier.

On the trading floor, a young Faith stops trying to adjust the bright silk jacket that is too tight and looks up at the chiming clock. Raven-sized carnivorous butterflies peck at the lining of her stomach but she is ready to start making her fortune, more than ready. She would grasp this opportunity with both hands, her feet, and any other part of her anatomy that was required.

Faith had vowed that she would never, ever, be poor again, never. Faith would die before going back to the streets. Being destitute in America was soul-destroying and, in Chicago, it was also freezing.

In Faith's darkest and almost final hour she had seen the light, had been blinded by it, temporarily. To this day she did not know why she had looked up from the poised pile of sleeping pills held in her icy hand. As she lifted her eyes, the sun had burst through the clouds. The polished glass of the Mercantile reflected and magnified the golden rays, searing Faith's being.

The flash of light broke the spell of suicide woven by the ghosts of a painful past. A deep rage was sparked within, and Faith was transformed from victim to predator. The market had called her, and she had responded. She could not explain it and had never tried.

Before the echo of the last chime fades Faith looks eagerly, and somewhat naively, around for trading opportunities. Of course, as a newbie, she starts at the bottom of the pit, the quietest part of the pit, the part of the pit furthest from easy action. Trading pits are aptly named. They are a cesspool of testosterone, cigarette smoke, foul BO, and fouler language.

The gold pit is the largest pit at the Mercantile, holding over 200 traders, but it is not buzzing that fateful morning. Desperate to start her career, Faith hustles and shouts tirelessly in a vain attempt

2

to make her first trade, two whole contracts. "God, what a joke", she thinks. Nervous about two contracts, but it was a lot back then and she hadn't eaten for days. Faith was hungrier than anyone else in the pit.

Being new is always difficult. In an environment, populated by a pack of part hyena alpha males, it is also meant to be humiliating. There was no need for a glass ceiling on the trading floors back then. Few females were brave or stupid enough to walk through the revolving entrance and those that did, exited so quickly that there was no need to push the door as it was always still spinning from their way in.

Faith is studiously ignored by the other traders. Well, that is not strictly true; her tits were not being ignored nor was her ass or the front of her ass. More comments were being swapped about Faith than contracts being traded. The remarks were loud, crass, and made mainly for the benefit of fellow buffoons.

Faith had heard worse, or equal anyway, so it didn't fuss her too much, but she was getting pissed off with the fact that with their eyes glued to her chest they wouldn't meet her eyes to make a trade. "Just one lousy trade to get started for Christ's sake," she thought.

Big Fat Bob did Faith a big fat favor that morning. Bob was the pit's prize smart ass. He was so fat he probably hadn't seen his dick in 20 years but that didn't stop it thinking for him. Seeing a woman, an attractive woman, OK, a very attractive woman, in the pit was just too much for Big Fat Bob.

Bob's comments were easily the loudest and though the competition for the crudest, stupidest thing to say was fierce, Bob won it easily. If only the men's comments could have been taped and played back for the enjoyment of their wives and children, perhaps their local pastor?

When a stupid man is surrounded and egged on by men of equal or greater ignorance, he can reach the pinnacle of his personal stupidity. Big Fat Bob peaked that morning.

Somehow it never dawned on him that Faith had not got lost and just wandered into the gold pit for his private entertainment. Faith knew it was going to be tough and that she would handle it. She could survive anything. Whilst there was lots of jostling, the men nearest Faith wisely gave her some space. They didn't trade with her, but they didn't try to grab a piece of her either.

From the corner of her eye, Faith sees Bob making suggestive gestures with his hips, much to the delight of his feeble-minded comrades. He then begins a mad pantomime of putting a latex glove on his big fat right hand, preparing himself to give Faith an "examination."

As the fat 'Doctor' begins to lumber down towards the bottom of the pit, Faith moves as if oblivious to her pending appointment. In fact, Faith positions herself and her *derrière* in such a way that Bob arrives on the pit tier directly above her.

Doc Bob pauses, partly to savor the moment, partly to draw further attention to him but mostly to gulp air into his heaving chest. Faith tenses, forcing herself to breathe deeply, all senses on high alert. The anticipatory snickering of the cronies tells Faith that Bob hopes to entertain the troops.

As Big Fat Bob bends down, Faith twists and uses his momentum to pull him forward. As he falls forward, Faith brings her knee up into his big fat nose, smashing it. Faith is careful to ensure that she is not trapped beneath the shocked, bleeding behemoth.

There is a collective intake of breath, the snickering cut off mid-snick, and for a moment, all breathing stops. Big Fat Bob lands badly and rolls onto his back, whimpering pathetically. His hands fly up to his shattered nose trying, too late, to protect it.

Faith does not look at Bob. She looks hard into the faces of the other traders in the pit. None of them hold her gaze.

Tap. Tap. Tap.

As Faith glares around the pit, she puts her hand out in front of her, palm up. Slowly, Faith curls her long, shiny, red nails inwards. Unable to break away, all eyes watch her, entranced. When Faith's talons finally touch, she pulls her hand down swiftly. The enchantment is broken and there is an involuntary wince from every pair of testicles in the pit as gonads try desperately to retreat upward into the safety of their owners' body cavity.

Knock. Knock. Knock.

Faith looks up to where Big Fat Bob had stood only moments before. There is no longer a space. Behind her Bob is moaning and trying to stand; no one helps him. Faith climbs the pit and like the Red Sea parting for Moses, a gap appears, and Faith takes Big Fat Bob's place. The traders are careful not to accidentally jostle her.

In the dog-eat-dog world of commodity trading, Faith had just lifted her leg on the pit and marked it as her own. The other dogs would never be Faith's friends, but they would wag their tails respectfully. To be successful, Faith wanted to be feared and respected, and thanks to Big Fat Bob, she achieved both in one morning. Big Fat Bob never returned to trading.

KNOCK, KNOCK, KNOCK, KNOCK.

The banging on the door brings Faith back to the present. Faith's hand is curled on her desk, her nails are still long, sharp, and bright red, but her skin is mottled and dry and no longer has the vibrancy of youth. Where had all the years gone? Faith's hand shakes and she frowns at it, but the knocking demands her attention.

"In the practice of tolerance, one's enemy is the best teacher." ~ Dalai Lama

Chapter 2

"Come in."

The door opens instantly and Cheryl marches in, carrying the bound reports for the board meeting. Cheryl: smart, serious, efficient and... plain. A generous person could describe her as, 'wholesome.' Her previous boss had not been generous, and she had been replaced by a woman with half her skills but twice her cleavage.

Faith had never seen Cheryl smile. Maybe she had forgotten how? Maybe she physically couldn't? Maybe not. It didn't matter. Cheryl was the best personal assistant she had ever had. Faith didn't care how Cheryl looked, what color she was, or anything else about her, as long as she excelled at her job. She did.

Cheryl looks at her boss as she puts the reports on the desk. Faith is looking tired, exhausted to her very core, which was her normal look these days. Cheryl grabs a tissue and hands it to Faith, pointing at her eye. Faith frowns. They say it takes 43 muscles to frown but only 17 muscles to smile. Faith's mouth had an almost permanent downturn to it. The effort for Faith to frown was minimal, four muscle movements at the most.

Faith rapidly repairs her make-up in front of a mirror. Cheryl tries to remember the last time she saw Faith coordinate the use of 17 muscles. Her search comes up blank.

Faith was appalling to work for. She had no sense of humor, was excruciatingly demanding, and kept horrendous hours. Essentially, Faith was a trading legend and a bitch, a legendary bitch. But on the other hand, Faith was always clear with her instructions and judged Cheryl only on the quality of her work which suited Cheryl just fine. Under Faith's strict guidance, Cheryl had made more money than she could have ever dreamed.

"Chuck was on the phone all last night to the good ol' boys, in Australia and South Africa. He's going to fight you, Faith, all the way ..." Faith finalizes fixing her war paint without responding. Lamely, Cheryl finishes, "But you already knew that."

One of Cheryl's early jobs for Faith was to establish an efficient information network in the City and within Napoleon Brothers. It was amazing what people would tell you if you asked, were respectful, and prepared to listen. If you also rewarded certain information, it was mind-blowing, and at times disturbing. Paying attention to people and sources that most traders ignored was one of the factors that contributed to Faith's success, but she had learned this lesson the hard way.

Ego, and not having access to soft data, had led to 'Faith's Folly,' as she called it. After exhaustive research, Faith had tried to manipulate silver prices and within a nightmarish 10 minutes, she had sustained a loss so colossal that it could have crippled her forever as a trader.

A white knight, Bernhard Napoleon, had miraculously bailed Faith out of her 'situation' and she had worked for Bernhard ever since. Trading with the backing of Napoleon Brothers had given Faith a much bigger dick to swing than if she had traded by herself. Swinging a 'big dick' was the parlance for a trader that could muster very large amounts of capital. Boys will be boys, unfortunately, and this was the only game where the size of the toy really mattered.

Faith snaps her compact mirror shut and addresses Cheryl. "Anyone surprising?" Cheryl shakes her head.

"No, no central bankers. Directors of the big miners, mainly. Apparently, he spent most of the time telling them his theories rather than listening to what they had to say." Faith smooths out the creases in her dark blue Armani pantsuit and throws back her shoulders.

"Thank God! If Chuck ever agreed with me, I would be very, very, worried... no, make that terrified." Faith takes the reports and heads to the boardroom for her final battle.

It seems to Faith that she had been fighting stupid white men her entire life. Did she hate her father when she was born? She was probably too exhausted to hate him then, though no doubt as an intelligent human being, albeit a small one, she would have cause to hate him shortly thereafter. Thinking of her father always made her a tougher adversary in the frequent, vicious clashes she had at Napoleon Brothers.

In a way, she th, she could almost thank her father. An involuntary snort at the sheer absurdity of that thought catches Faith off guard and the stack of reports threatens to spill onto the floor of the elevator. Hell would have to be crushed by a glacier for an epoch before that happened. Faith always thought big; hell freezing over as an analogy would never occur to her. The lift door opens. As Faith steps over the threshold, her breathing quickens.

The boardroom of Napoleon Brothers spoke of old money and privilege, heavy oil paintings, and dark mahogany timber. There were no mounted animal heads on the walls, not anymore, but the smoke from a thousand stogies had stained the ceiling.

The company's 'No Smoking' policy did not apply to the upper echelons of Napoleon Brothers. A life-size portrait of Bernhard Napoleon looms large over the head of the table. Reclined beneath the portrait is the man himself; his Italian-made black leather cowboy boots rest contemptuously on the table.

From behind half-closed eyes, Bernhard surveys his kingdom. The reclined posture, hands templed on his midriff, creates unease amongst the Directors, as it is meant to. Bernhard loves watching the jockeying, the preening, the frequent furtive glances his way.

Much of the boardroom behavior, the strutting, sparring and the put-downs are done to impress him, but no one is ever quite sure whether Bernhard is paying attention. Bernhard's impassive expression provides no feedback whilst the eyes from his portrait seem to follow every move. Of course, they didn't follow every move; the cameras installed in the lighting system did that.

The thought of having cameras in the eyes of his portrait did appeal to Bernhard but, unfortunately, it was too Scooby-Doo for him to ever "doo" it. God, he hated Scooby-Doo. Bernhard had had a dog that once ran from the pig they were hunting. He'd shot the cowardly dog in front of the other dogs and let the pig go.

You weren't allowed to shoot executives who ran from a fight, even in Texas, but you could humiliate them and fire their sorry asses. At some point in their career, every board member had witnessed or been shamed in this very room.

The whole elaborate charade was orchestrated to create uncertainty and fear. Fear, Bernhard had learned, was a powerful motivating tool, and in the markets, if a man, or woman, could not control their fear they were useless, weak, dead meat.

Bernhard watches Faith as she enters the room. Much of the banter ceases. Across the room, Bernhard can see Chuck's eyes narrow, his nostrils flare and his lips pull back from his teeth.

It takes all of Bernhard's considerable self-control not to chortle. He loved observing Chuck. He was so pure in his loathing of Faith. Bernhard only wished that he could take credit for fostering the feeling in some small way but, alas, it had been hate at first sight.

Bernhard did take credit for using Chuck as a constant thorn in Faith's side, manipulating Faith's abhorrence of Chuck for good instead of evil. Good for Bernhard Napoleon anyway.

Faith was an exceptional trader; an uncanny trader and Bernhard had spotted her early in her career when Faith's ability was limited only by her capital. Bernhard had promptly offered Faith a job, a highly lucrative, senior position at Napoleon Brothers. He had not been surprised; indeed, he had been pleased, when Faith had firmly turned him down.

Faith was a lone wolf. She answered to no one and her reputation grew quickly. Bernhard knew that if he waited too long, he would be unable to 'secure' her services. Unbeknownst to the general market, Napoleon Brothers had too often been on the wrong side of a raging bull market. They were exposed and desperately needed a gifted and bold trader. They needed Faith.

Unfortunately, lone wolves do not understand the power of a strong pack. They have no reference for the support a pack can bring which means it is a weakness, a blind spot. Bernhard had been an alpha male for a long time, as had his father before him. He still had the scars from when he had taken over his father's pack. Bernhard's pack was extensive, influential, and ruthless. Keeping them in line was not without its risks.

It took all of Bernhard's cunning, a dash of violence, the calling in of long-held favors and the flouting of several National Securities Commission laws, plus a few domestic ones, to financially trap Faith. Napoleon Brothers was her only way out of mind-crippling debt and probably a prison sentence.

Bernhard was particularly proud of the fact that he had achieved this without Faith ever discovering that he was behind the astonishing short run on silver that had almost resulted in Faith's biggest play being her last.

The beautiful irony of it all was that Napoleon Brothers made more that day than they had made in the previous six months.

When Faith joined Napoleon Brothers shortly after the wild fluctuations, the market gave her credit for the success of her "bold tactic." Bernhard encouraged this perception and thus was "Faith's Folly," as only Bernhard and Faith referred to it, transformed into one of Faith's early market coups.

After a last spray of spittle, Chuck pauses to take a deep breath. He had to. His lungs were screaming for air and passing out mid-tirade is invariably considered bad form. Winning arguments with volume was a tactic that Chuck had used successfully to get him what he wanted his whole life. But he knew from bitter experience that shouting did not intimidate Faith McCormack, nor did his towering 6-foot-4 frame. Against Faith, a mere woman, Chuck rarely won, and it infuriated him. He could feel his ulcer flare up, but he ignored it. Chuck had mastered ignorance a long time ago.

Softly now, dangerously softly, Chuck addresses Faith directly, "You have been extraordinarily lucky. I'll give you that, eah? But ..." Chuck faces the room, raises his voice, and saturates it with venom, "Everybody's luck runs out, eventually. What you are proposing is insane. Insane! It will ruin us!" Chuck slaps Faith's report dramatically on the table as he rises to his full height.

Faith could feel her gorge rising and a part of, quite a big part of her, wanted to scream back at Chuck. Whilst temporarily satisfying, she knew that that strategy would not get her what she wanted, and Faith wanted this. Faith wanted this so badly that instead of screaming she uses the scythe that is her tongue. "The ignorant and lazy believe in luck, Chuck, so it's no surprise that you are a paragon of the powers of chance. I get the results I get through sheer hard work."

Chuck's nostrils become mere slits. He fights to maintain control. "Boo, hoo, hoo, poor Faith always working so hard. Maybe if you had a life you wouldn't have to work so hard? Eah?"

Chuck could see that the arrow had hit home. A snigger escapes from one of the Directors. Chuck pounces to deliver his coup de grace: "Gold is as low as it will ever get. It has bottomed. The biggest miners in the world told me that they are now long or were you doing your nails when I explained that?"

The remark about not having a life had stung. Faith felt the pain of loneliness and to have it thrust in her face by a man she despised was cruel. The familiar sexist comment was a relief. Faith looks at Chuck. He was quite pathetic, not worth getting upset over.

"The fact that these men waste their time gossiping with you, Chucky, tells me everything I need to know about their intelligence, integrity, and work ethic." Faith turns away from Chuck and addresses the rest of the board.

"Are there any intelligent objections?"

Chuck flushes. He knows he is right this time. He had the inside run. When the Directors of the largest gold miners in the world tell him something, he listens. Chuck was a market and religious fundamentalist. He had no time for fancy charts. If Chuck's sources had stopped selling into the world market and were now starting to forward buy, then gold had only one way it could go - up. God, he was looking forward to rubbing that smug bitch's face in this one.

"If you are so sure, why don't you back it with your own money?" sneers Chuck. As soon as he says this, he realizes his error, but it is too late. Faith does not bat an eyelid, her mouth twitches into the faintest of smiles. She stares back at Chuck until he has to break away. "I am, Chucky, with everything I've got, and if you had testicles bigger than your tonsils, you'd do the same. Let the market determine which one of us is right."

Faith watches the impact of her words and savors the setting of the highly honed and public hook in the foul mouth of this prime Texan redneck. Faith puts on a fake Panhandle accent and flutters her eyelids "Or do you have to ask ... Yo' big ol' Daddy's permission first?"

Chuck swallows the hook, the rod, and then the boat. Mocking his father was too much for Chuck. He turns purple with rage before he loses control. Some men will never hit a woman, no matter what the provocation. Chuck had never been limited by such sexist scruples.

In Chuck's world, there were times when both men and women deserved to be hit and this was such an occasion and, by God, Chuck was not going to pull the blow. Bernhard finally breaks his silence when Chuck is halfway around the table.

"Charles!"

One word, but the spoken equivalent of a magnum being fired. Chuck stops mid-charge. His eyes do not leave Faith. His desire to quench his thirst for violence radiates from him. Faith tries not to smirk, but just for a moment, and then she indulges herself in the most annoying smug look she has in her arsenal. Bernhard is motionless, his eyes still closed but the room waits... and waits.

"Faith?" The question is a command. Faith waves the folder in front of her as Chuck sulkily slumps back into his seat. "I have never seen such a strong setup. Wake up and smell the blood gentlemen…"

At the mention of the word 'blood,' Bernhard opens his eyes. He looks intently at Faith. Faith continues, "There is a killing to be made and we have no more time. Delay any longer and we will never get positioned. It could take years to make the same profit we can make in the next few days."

The room is silent. Bernhard raises his eyebrow, it is almost imperceptible, but it is enough for Faith to keep going. "I have cycles for gold coming in that date back to Roman times. Technically it is the strongest setup I have ever seen," Faith pauses, "and my gut is screaming 'go for it.'" Shocked gasps follow this statement. No trader but Faith would dare to mention the force of a 'gut feeling,' it was too intangible, ephemeral, unquantifiable, and unmasculine.

Faith alone knows that Bernhard has enormous respect for her intuition. Faith's final card is on the table. She sits down and leans back. It was done. In theory, there should be a vote now but, in practice, only one person would determine the direction of the board. Bernhard starts to smile or at least the edges of his mouth move upwards. He has thin lips, and his smiles are more reptilian than human. There is nothing warm in Bernhard. The smile never reaches his unblinking eyes.

Slowly, deliberately, Bernhard Napoleon removes first one polished boot and then the other from the boardroom table. He stands up and leans forward. One by one he stares at each person in the room. No one, not even Faith, can hold his gaze.

Finally, Bernhard delivers his pronouncement. "Well, Gen'lmen, looks like we got a whole lot of selling to do, eah?" Bernhard slowly resumes his reclined position. His boots make a loud thud as they land back on the table.

Faith is relieved but she hides it. Publicly she gloats and, as she stares scornfully at Chuck, she massages her brow with just her middle finger. If livid was a color, then Chuck's face goes a deep livid. It is childish of Faith to give Chuck the finger that way but deeply, deeply gratifying. This was going to be the biggest play of a career of big plays. Game on.

Outside the warm office, it has started to snow. Big, fluffy, white flakes sail silently past the window. A few pioneer flakes land on Faith's windowsill waiting for frozen backup which does not come quickly enough. But each ice crystal that hits the ledge makes it easier for the next snowflake to last a little longer. It is a beautiful crystalline dance. The snow should tell someone who cares.

"Markets are constantly in a state of uncertainty and flux and money is made by discounting the obvious and betting on the unexpected." ~ George Soros

Chapter 3

Faith types rapidly on her laptop, glancing up frequently to check the constantly updating data from the screens that surround her office desk. The sun is struggling to lighten the horizon. The clouds are so thick that the sun could give up and take the day off and no one would even notice. Faith pauses briefly to stab at her intercom, "Update."

Cheryl tries to hide the worry from her voice. "We've sold 3,012 contracts... aaaand we are down over 18 million and the losses are accelerating."

Faith's voice through the intercom sounds like a robot, even more like a robot than usual, thinks a tired Cheryl. The intercom barks into life again.

"You have let the market know it is me selling?" Cheryl stares at the gold chart on one of her screens.

"Yes, I did that ...and... um, it only made it worse this time." Faith can hear Cheryl's mounting concern, and in her inimical style, she addresses it.

"Nut up woman." The intercom clicks off. There is a reason why robots are not used in counseling services.

Faith's computer pings, indicating a new email. Faith glances at the calendar open on her desktop. Every day starts at 6:00 AM and finishes after 10:00 PM. She types a note to herself, "Remember to pick up a life on the way home."

After she closes her calendar, she checks the new message. It is from Bernhard. It is URGENT. It is terse. "SEE ME ON ARRIVAL!" Faith types, "I never left, resistance expected. Many hate me for my success and being a woman. Chuck is not alone in wanting to see me fail. C u in 10."

Faith's hand clenches on the mouse, her finger poised above the left click button, it shakes as she hesitates. She changes the 10 to a 5 and savagely presses Send.

Night follows day, as it must, unaffected by the machinations of the market. Chicago under streetlights is muffled by a thickening layer of once-white snow. The Napoleon Brothers' office is a red-hot hub of activity.

Faith stifles a yawn as she stares at a one-minute spot gold chart. Adrenalin can only take you so far. Even Faith needed a little sleep every 48 hours. It was unprecedented to hold such a large position for so long. Fortunately, the price of gold was softening. It was an incredibly bold move. A recently rested Cheryl is talking animatedly into her headset.

Faith grabs her handbag and heads out the door. Faith doesn't wait for Cheryl to finish her call; as she passes her she says, "I'm going to catch a little sleep – ring me if anything happens. Did you get through to Mike?"

Cheryl looks up at Faith and nods her head. She flips down her mouthpiece to respond, but Faith has already swept past, wrapping her saffron scarf around her neck as she walks to the lift. The scarf Faith is wearing is the same color as...

... As the shapeless robes of a Tibetan Buddhist acolyte, Tenzin, that flap in the bitterly cold Himalayan wind. Icicles hang off the bottom of the pair of binoculars that Tenzin is intently looking through.

Tenzin's magnified gaze sweeps over snow-covered mountain peaks and into a distant valley. The focus zooms in and out. Ant-like specks crystallize into people, then into blurs, then back into people again. The figures all look similar. With a tweak of the fine focus, a recurring red splash becomes discernible. Tenzin cannot see it clearly but knows what it is. The splash of color is a red star logo with a yellow outline. The People's Liberation Army would not call it a logo but a symbol. In Tibet, that symbol is one of repression and genocide, not liberation.

Transfixed, Tenzin's breathing gets faster and shallower. Finally, with a shudder, the binoculars are lowered. A thickly gloved hand brushes the icicles away. The eyepieces of the binoculars have left two ice-free regions on Tenzin's face. The eyes that peer out do not look quite right. Tenzin's right eye is dark brown, the left eye is blue. *Heterochromia iridium* is the scientific name for two different colored eyes in an individual. Freak, devil's spawn, and retard were the non-scientific names.

A sudden snapping sound comes from the lines of colorful prayer flags that radiate from a small tent staked out in the lee of the little shelter that was available. Sitting in a perfect lotus position on the exposed ledge in front of the tent is an old monk, a very old monk, Khenchen Chodha, the ex-Abbot of Sera Monastery. He is silent and motionless. His thread-worn saffron robes and bare left shoulder are highly incongruous with the freezing surroundings. The ledge overlooks the most sacred lake in Tibet, Lhamo Latso, the 'Oracle Lake.'

It is said that the Goddess Palden Lhamo, the principal protectress of Tibet and the guardian spirit of the lake, came to the 1st Dalai Lama, Gendun Drup (1391 to 1474) in a vision and promised that she would protect the reincarnation lineage of the Dalai Lamas.

Regent Reting received the vision that led him to the discovery of the 14th Dalai Lama, Tenzin Gyatso whilst overlooking Lhamo Latso in 1935. His Holiness was only three years old when he first met Regent Reting.

Previous regents had also received visions from the sacred water. The lake's history of granting visions to those who meditate upon its surface made it popular with tourists in the warmer months. But given the lake's power and importance in Tibetan history, it was now strictly off-limits to Tibetan monks or nuns or… any Tibetan.

Visions were unpredictable and could not be controlled by the Chinese authorities of the highly autocratic and non-autonomous Tibetan Autonomous Region, the TAR. The Chinese do not want or need a vision to find the 15th Dalai Lama. They have chosen him already. A couple times. But the current one was getting older and if the 14th Dalai Lama did not die soon; they would have to choose again.

Under the dark, cloudy sky the skull-shaped lake appears murky, unfathomable. Ripples of wind race each other across the surface. The snow is still falling, thick flakes that cover everything… almost everything. There is no snow on the Abbot or on a small circular patch of ground around him.

Tenzin breathes in the thin air, making use of a thick chuba jacket to stay warm and Buddhist training to remain calm. Almost calm. Given the circumstances, it was a great result and a testimony to a gifted teacher.

The news of their impending visitors was crucial information, but disturbing the Abbot to tell him, that was not an option. Tenzin knew one thing for certain; worrying was not going to help. After picking up a cushion, Tenzin sits lithely in the lotus position and becomes still, opening to the bliss that radiated from Kenchen.

A black cloud casts a dragon-like shadow that flits across the calm surface of the lake.

"When I played in the sandbox, the cat kept covering me up." ~ *Rodney Dangerfield*

Chapter 4

Fluffy, an ungrateful and unimaginatively named Khao Manee cat, is curled up in her basket in Faith's pristine penthouse. Fluffy's different colored eyes are both closed. The pure white Khao Manee was the royal cat breed of Old Siam, and it is said that the penalty for a commoner stealing one was death, which might help explain why Fluffy behaves as if she is a queen. It may also be because she is a cat.

The interior designer-designed décor, the magnificent views over Lake Michigan, and the expensive kitty litter are all wasted on Fluffy. The large sickly pot plant, on the other hand, was being wasted by the cat. Hidden behind thick curtains, the new day was dawning.

A discordant untidy trail of women's clothing leads from the immaculate lounge room to the bedroom. Silent witnesses, the trading screens scattered throughout the apartment flicker with unending updates. Unlike any human the market never sleeps, it just moves around the globe from one trading zone to the next.

Faith is awake before her alarm. Still asleep next to her is Mike. Mike is handsome and well-muscled but in a yummy yoga kind of way rather than a 'my arms can't touch the side of my body' weights kind of way. Faith rolls onto her side and stares at Mike.

A loud, crass, KA-CHING, KA-CHING ringtone from the bedside table shatters the silence and jerks Faith out of her brief revelry. She quickly snatches up the phone. It is a breathless Cheryl.

"Just came through. Bank of England is about to make an announcement on gold reserves. It's starting to tank."

Energy surges through Faith as she tells Cheryl, "This is it! It's buying time, start closing out our positions. I'm on my way."

Faith hangs up and allows herself a rare smile that transforms her face from formidable to beautiful. It doesn't last because her brain gets in the way. If a central bank was buying, they generally did it quietly, to keep the acquisition price down. If they were making a market announcement it could only mean one thing, they were about to reduce their gold reserves as other reserve banks had done recently. Stupidity was the common currency of central banks and Faith had cashed a lot more than her fair share of checks from them.

Long ago Faith had stopped trying to predict the how or why mechanisms of major market movements. All that mattered was getting the 'when' and the 'which way' right. She revered the legendary trader W.D. Gann's way of analyzing cycles within cycles. Though Gann had died in 1955, Faith had managed to track down and buy many of his original charts and his data.

Faith's steel discipline, and exhaustive research combined with a rigorous methodology, had served her remarkably well… except, except for her first big trade which had gone spectacularly wrong.

Stops were missed, instructions to liquidate positions had not been followed, and the broker's automatic phone recording system that should have recorded and corroborated her market instructions had inexplicably been on the blink. Even stops that should not have been hit were hit. It had nearly ruined her and if she had gone to prison it would have killed her. One day she would go back and have another look at that whole mess. There was something odd about it but there was also a lot of pain in revisiting it, so she never had.

Mike starts to stir, and Faith turns back to look at him but the moment, if indeed it had been a moment, has passed. Faith slaps Mike sharply on the butt as she leaps out of the bed and makes for the shower.

A startled Mike watches Faith as she closes the glass shower door behind her and turns on the water. He gets out of bed and dresses quickly, efficiently. As he straightens his silk tie, he picks up the brown envelope with his name on it from the top of the dresser and slips it inside his custom-made suit jacket.

Mike faces Faith who has disappeared in a cloud of steam. He makes an elaborate courtier bow and lets himself out. Mike is a true gentleman.

Minutes later, a power-dressed Faith emerges from the bedroom. The flush in her cheeks is not from makeup; it is the warm glow of sweet righteousness spiced with the anticipation of humiliating Chuck. The trail of clothes is sitting in a neat pile on the couch. Mike was not just a gentleman; he was tidy as well. There were not many men like Mike around. Faith knew she was lucky; he was worth every dollar.

Faith picks up her Ferrari keys and goes to open the lounge room curtains to let the first rays of the sun enter the apartment, if there were any rays. The pot plant certainly looked like it needed some light. As she touches the curtains she stumbles clumsily and bangs her head hard against the sliding glass doors behind them.

When she looks up, her dark brown eyes have become as hard and cold as the falling snow.

"Nearly all men can stand adversity, but if you want to test a man's character, give him power." ~
Abraham Lincoln

Chapter 5

It is snowing heavily, and the light is fading fast. Low cloud obscures the high grey mountains that have been tucked under a fresh but icy white blanket.

Despite the 5,300-meter altitude, the steep slope, and the severe weather, the Chinese soldiers are closer. They would be thoroughly pissed off at having been forced out of their warm, relatively oxygen-rich, Lhasa barracks to chase an old Tibetan.

The tent in the hollow is no longer there. The camp has been packed into one large, bulging backpack except for a dented, blackened metal teapot that sits on a ring of rocks over a weakly smoldering fire.

The alternating blue, white, red, green, and yellow prayer flags provide welcome splashes of color in the otherwise bleak environment. Every snap and flutter of fabric, every breath of wind that passes over the printed mantras takes the prayers to every crack and corner of the universe. Prayers that ask for the end of suffering for all sentient beings… all beings… regardless of the logo on their clothing.

Khenchen Chodha has not moved. Despite a concerted effort, the snow still fails to settle on him. The old monk was the greatest living adept of tummo. Tummo is a highly advanced and profoundly deep tantric meditation practice that produces body heat as a side effect of meditation.

Among Tibetans, this man was a priceless living treasure. Many years ago, he had been beaten, stripped of his position as Abbot, and imprisoned for the heinous crime of being caught possessing a picture of his friend and ex-pupil, the Dalai Lama.

He was one of a rapidly dwindling number of lamas schooled and brought up in Tibet prior to the 1950 Chinese invasion. He laughed frequently, often at himself. He was a humble, joyous man, a patient tutor, and the holder of teachings that Tenzin was hoping to record so they would not be lost forever. Just to be in his presence was a teaching in itself.

Tenzin pours steaming yak's milk and rancid butter tea into a cup which is then grasped tightly in both hands, hands that shake, not just from the cold.

Even in bright morning sunlight Bernard's office always seemed like a dark place to Faith. Outside it was cloudy again, so it was even grimmer than usual.

Holding the gold-leaf-adorned glass in both hands, Faith waits for Bernhard to remove the stopper from the bottle that sits in its unique hand-crafted aluminum and glass chest. Bernhard has noticed the way Faith is trying to keep her hands steady. Of course he notices.

He takes the glass from Faith and carefully, reverently pours some amber liquid in before he hands it back. It would never do to spill even a drop of the *Hennessy Beauté du Siècle Cognac*.

At a price of over $13 per drop or $200,000 for a single bottle that would be wasteful, and Bernhard was not wasteful. Extravagant? Absolutely. Wasteful, no. There were occasions that warranted extreme extravagance to add proper gravitas to the celebrations. This was one of those occasions. There was also something wickedly delicious in making obscene amounts of money and paying a lower tax rate than a man struggling to pay off a modest mortgage. God Bless America!

Faith frowns as she twirls the cognac in her glass. She pauses to admire the color and the bouquet. Bernhard stands in front of Faith and lifts his glass so they can toast. The lead crystal clinking lead crystal produces a crisp clean note that lingers in the air.

After taking a sip Bernhard remarks, "Post-killing nerves, eah? Not like you." Faith smiles weakly before she drops the pretense of smiling. She takes a careful sip, savoring it.

Faith was not celebrating. She was not very good at it at the best of times, and this should have been the best of best times. She had just planted her flag on the highest peak of a Himalaya-like career. Today was a triumph, but it didn't seem to be. Bernhard found this annoying and... puzzling.

"I've always wondered, eah? Was it abhorrence at first sight with Chuck? Or did your repulsion develop over time?"

Faith does not respond. She tries to decide whether to play the familiar game of cat and mouse with Bernhard or to surprise him with an honest answer. She did not feel safe opening up to Bernhard, but she was bone-weary of the constant pretense, so it was difficult. Finally, she drags her gaze off her glass and looks Bernhard in the eyes. Even so, she hesitates and draws a deep breath before she replies. "He reminds me of my father."

There is a pregnant silence. There was no light-hearted quip to that answer. Bernhard likes to know everyone's secrets so he can exploit them, but he does not like people opening up to him. It makes him uncomfortable.

Bernhard breaks eye contact. He turns and carefully places the elegant bottle back into its superbly designed stand. When he twists to face Faith again, he lifts his glass.

"To our first billion-dollar day!"

Faith lifts her glass and throws back the rest of her cognac in a calculated $7,000 gulp that she knows will piss Bernhard off. She turns her back on him and looks out the window at the sparkling city below.

Stifling his annoyance, Bernhard asks, "Is there anything I can offer you to make you stay this time?"

Faith continues to stare out the window. Slowly she turns. "Bernhard, nothing you can say could keep me in this human cesspool any longer. Nothing." Faith looks drained of life essence as she holds her glass in both hands to dampen the shaking. This time it is Faith who lowers her eyes.

Bernhard never took 'no,' for an answer. During his college years, this had gotten him into trouble with a girlfriend or four, but none had dared press charges. Fortunately for Bernhard, in business, never taking a 'no' was considered a virtue.

Trying to lighten the mood he grins and this time he pours on all of his considerable charisma. Surprisingly, Bernhard could be quite charming when he tried to be. But he had had so much power for so long that he didn't need to try very often. "But what will you do Faith? ... If you leave."

Faith starts a justification routine. "Bernhard, I am going to do lots of things, like..." But she falters, "like..."

Never having given the question sufficient consideration makes a confident performance in front of an unsympathetic crowd quite difficult.

Faith sighs. "Me? Do? I don't know exactly... But what I do know is this, I want to start to enjoy my wealth, enjoy my life. I feel like I'm dying here." She doesn't exactly nail her dismount which leaves Bernhard with an opening.

Adopting a fatherly tone, Bernhard silkily strokes Faith's ego, "But Faith you are the only natural I have ever come across in this business. I am so proud of you. Trading is your gift. Just one more year, Faith. Just one more."

Faith shakes her head.

"Bernhard, I'm 40, I'm retiring."

"One more year and I'll give you what you've always wanted, my job and Chuck's head. By the way, Chuck's father refused to let him use any of the family money to invest against you."

There is a very long pause. Faith inspects her empty glass. Bernhard clears his throat. "Faith?"

"Six months, maybe, while I work out what I want to do. But I want more than Chuck's head, Bernhard. I want his balls." To emphasize the point, she curls her fingernails in and makes a swift castration movement with her hand. "And I want his daddy's financial balls too. I want them fiscally neutered, totally wiped out."

Bernhard looks at Faith, his face an expressionless mask. No trace of the triumph shows nor his sudden concern for his own well-being. Faith was a bad enemy to have. Note to self; destroy any shred of evidence that could reveal my clandestine involvement in 'Faith's Folly.' Bernhard was too old for a new enemy like Faith.

He drains the last sip from his glass, relishing the exquisite taste. It was as close to drinking money as you could get.

"You should know that Chuck's father is an old... acquaintance of mine. One of my oldest... acquaintances..."

As he is speaking Bernhard carefully refills his glass. He holds it up to the light and swirls it around admiring the way the precious liquid is illuminated in the pure crystal. After taking a moment to sniff the delicate scent, he reluctantly sets his glass down on the table.

"Of course, Chuck's ego, greed, and temper make him easy prey, childishly easy... and business always comes before acquaintanceships. Done!"

Bernhard walks over to Faith with the poised bottle while he holds out his free hand to shake on the deal that he had not expected to get.

Instead of sealing the deal or accepting a $15,000 to $20,000 top-up, Faith places her empty glass in Bernhard's outstretched hand. "I said, maybe. I'll let you know," and with that Faith turns and walks out the door.

Her knees wobble. She tells herself that it is just nerves.

"The teacher who is indeed wise does not bid you to enter the house of his wisdom but rather leads you to the threshold of your mind." ~ *Khalil Gibran*

Chapter 6

The poor light makes it difficult to see. Despite this, with small, precise, strokes Khenchen Chodha finishes writing on a small piece of parchment. He considers his work and smiles, satisfied. Slowly, deliberately, he rolls the scroll and gives it to Tenzin who is nervous and impatient to be away.

"Read it, memorize it. Every word is priceless."

Down the hill, less than a mile away, light from several cook stoves can be seen. There is no firewood because there are no trees, and the PLA does not like to carry yak dung for fuel when they can have disposable butane cookers. Sadly, empty canisters would be frozen into the ground tomorrow.

The wizened old monk looks up at Tenzin and takes a deep, deep breath. Tears glisten in the wrinkly corners of his sparkling eyes and freeze. He continues in Tibetan, "The Oracle Lake has not failed us. I have had a remarkable vision, a prophecy."

In a voice that is not his own he says, "When the incarnation of the Dakini marked by the tear of the dragon is found by her mirror, the chains of the dragon will melt from the land of snows."

Each word sears into Tenzin's mind and into the surrounding rocks, snow, and flags. The prayer flags would chant the words of the prophecy into the wind until the last faded thread found flight. The frozen water crystals quietly add the energy of the vision to their crystalline structure. The waters of the world would also whisper the words of light and hope when the snows melted.

Khenchen takes Tenzin's hands and gently says, "The future of a free Tibet may well rest with you."

In Tenzin's face, he sees fear race towards panic. "Aroosh-Na-Ba," which means 'little one,' "Worry not; the protectors of this land will be with you and so will I, in spirit. You must take this to India, to the Tibetan Government in Exile in Dharamsala. They will know what to do... It must not fall into Chinese hands. If anything should happen... destroy it first." He smiles and the ice crystals around his eyes crackle.

Tenzin frowns. "In spirit? But you are coming with me. You have to. We can deliver it together."

The monk's smile never wavers but his eyes emphatically say 'no.' Tenzin becomes distraught. "But Rinpoche you must come with me. Rinpoche, they will punish you for coming here. Prison, beatings... they will kill you this time. Please, I can carry you. I am strong enough."

The ex-abbot stops Tenzin from lifting him. He takes Tenzin's head in his rough, sun-beaten hands and pulls it towards him until they touch foreheads. After a few moments, the Abbot pulls back and looks deep into Tenzin's eyes.

How remarkable, he thinks, that he should have brought Tenzin with him to this place on this sacred pilgrimage. He had seen Tenzin with him here in a dream long before they had met. Aaaa cha, a beautiful soul, a good choice.

Suddenly, he smiles again, laughs and shakes his head.

"The Chinese will find only my smiling shell here and maybe not much of that. I feel incredibly blessed. I have seen the future. I have seen my beloved Tibet free once more."

The Abbot's tears flow freely now, flowing too freely to freeze on his face. They fall on his robes as ice rather than droplets. He takes a special pouch from around his neck which holds his personal seal and hands it to Tenzin. The seal left in Sera Monastery was not authentic but there were only a few people in the world that would know the difference.

After a brief blessing, he beckons Tenzin to go. The wind was changing direction and the snow was turning to a drizzle. The waters of the world would not wait until spring to murmur the words of the prophecy. It was time to go. It was actually well after time to leave but Tenzin finds she cannot leave her guru.

Firmly the Abbot says, "They are very near. If you trust me, you must go now! Your path will not be easy but the Lady of the Lake, Palden Lhamo, and I will guide and protect you."

Distant voices can now be heard. Reluctantly, extremely reluctantly, Tenzin shoulders the backpack and sets off in the direction of Samye Monastery. Despite the risk of imprisonment, there would be help there for her.

Even for experienced mountaineers, it would be easy to get lost and die in these remote mountains. For novices… Unfortunately, Tenzin has no choice but to walk off, alone.

The clouds that have been hovering above the peak descend. The wind howls and the ledge disappears in a sea of white.

*"There is no such thing as accident; it is fate
misnamed."* ~ *Napoleon Bonaparte*

Chapter 7

The white glossy walls of the executive car park reflect the powerful LED lighting. Visitors to this shiny, highly secure enclave of exclusive cars were not welcome.

Faith's immaculate, designer boots wobble unsteadily as she approaches her vintage Ferrari. The shade of her red lipstick perfectly matches the color of the car. A welcoming beep greets her as she approaches. It would be purring soon enough. Faith gives the car one of her rare smiles. It was nice to have her driver's license back.

She reclines for a moment in the leather driver's seat. This is followed by more moments because her hand is shaking so much that she struggles to get the key into the ignition. She is so tired. The insignificant effort of turning the key in the ignition exhausts her.

"God, I am so out of practice! One drink! One, one-hundred-year-old drink." Whilst not a teetotaler, Faith was not a big drinker, mainly because she refused to drink alone.

Faith rests her head briefly on the steering wheel. The sound of the engine soothes her. When she backs out, she backs out fast. She would put her seatbelt on, later.

Some do-gooder had placed a large sign on the solid, burnished steel car park exit gate. That it had appeared after a pedestrian had been run over nearby was purely coincidental. It was a simple sign. It said, 'Drive Safely' and underneath that adage, there was an image of a mobile phone inside a red circle with a line across it. It conveniently reminds Faith to make a call. She immediately rummages in her bag and retrieves her phone. As she accelerates the wheels give a satisfying screech.

Faith drives with her mobile in the crook of her neck. She had upgraded her phone recently and it did not want to sync with her hands-free system.

Amber traffic lights to Faith mean accelerate. Red means floor it. She guns it to overtake a truck, swerving back into her lane just before the oncoming traffic. Faith gave women drivers a bad name which is strange because she drove like a man... a madman.

Under the harsh lights of a grey concrete military base, a snow-covered troop carrier pulls to a halt. The icy back flap of the truck rolls up from the inside. Two soldiers jump out and shout angrily into the back of the truck. Awkwardly, painfully, a maroon-clad figure climbs out and is soon surrounded by half a dozen half-frozen soldiers. Tenzin's shoulders are slumped; face and clothes are torn and bloody.

One of the soldiers jabs his rifle butt hard into Tenzin's back before they push their captive roughly towards a grimy and grim-looking building. It is an even grimmer-looking building than the other grey grim-looking buildings that make up the compound. A Jeep with an orange revolving light mounted on the roof drives past. It casts a crazy strobe effect on the razor wire fences and on Tenzin.

The flashing light from the top of the ambulance pierces the Chicago darkness and gives the crash scene a surreal feel. A crumpled red Ferrari is wrapped around a light pole. It is no longer purring.

Competent concerned paramedics carefully, but quickly, load a stretcher into the back of the ambulance. The doors close, the siren wails and the ambulance pulls swiftly away.

"Denial ain't just a river in Egypt." ~ *Mark Twain*

Chapter 8

Immersed in a thick, soupy fog, Faith feels like she is sinking, drowning. She is so exhausted. She can barely muster the strength to stay upright. When the fog swirls and thins, in a desperate bid to swim free, Faith drains the last of her energy reserves. Her legs kick frantically and her arms thrash and, just for a moment, she bursts above the fog.

In the hospital bed where she remains motionless Faith's eyes blink, but they refuse to register any of the details of the intensive care ward.

Too shattered to keep moving, Faith falls back into the fog. The brief eye flicker is enough to create great excitement in the hungry, white-coated vultures that perch around her.

A specialist in brain neurology and self-importance, Dr. Kleinstein immediately shines his pencil torch into the woman's eyes. His colleague and sycophant, Dr. Todd, almost drops the patient chart that he has been puzzling over.

Faith is a fighter. She somehow rallies again, making painfully slow but steady headway until the fog is suddenly blasted away. It becomes painfully bright, so she swiftly dives back into the safety of the welcoming depths of darkness.

"I agree with you, Doctor. This EEG is very strange." Dr. Kleinstein acknowledges the expected consensus with the briefest nod of his head. Disappointed by the lack of response by the comatose body, he puts his torch away extends his hand, and takes another look at the quickly proffered chart. "Those idiots downstairs probably made a mistake or gave us the wrong chart.

Have them run it again and check the CAT scan too. This can't be right."

A day later, Faith finally makes it through the fog long enough to briefly gain consciousness. Her face is bandaged and badly bruised.

Faith's reputation as a difficult patient preceded her to the ICU though it needn't have bothered. Faith had terrorized this hospital once every year for ten years as a consequence of the Napoleon Brothers' policy that insisted that all senior personnel have an annual physical.

The staff used a reverse lottery system to determine who saw her. All the physicians' names were put into a hat. One by one the names were pulled out, the last name left in the hat was the 'winner.' Doctors were not allowed to pull sickies just to get out of it. Somehow Faith had missed last year's physical and, funnily enough, no one at the hospital had rung her to reschedule.

As soon as she is able to speak, the doctors pummel her with questions. She doesn't answer them very well as she finds it incredibly difficult to concentrate. Everything is a bit blurry, and she is irritable, more irritable than normal.

"Jesus! Are you two deaf? I told you. I was exhausted. I'd had a drink that didn't agree with me. I don't remember anything else. It was an unfortunate accident. Like your birth."

Dr. Kleinstein is highly offended; he is not used to being talked to the way he deserves to be talked to. In a slightly higher voice than he intends, he responds. "Well… Ms. McCormack, it may have been just an accident. However, we have to be absolutely sure… as your…"

Slowly, but not patiently, Faith interjects. "It was an accident."

Dr. Todd comes to the defense of his famous colleague. He accidentally blurts out, "Well, maybe not. Your CT scan is anomalous. We need to do a brain biopsy."

The look she gives the trembling Todd could cook a roast. Then all the color drains from Faith's face making the purple bruises blacken. The possibility that it was not just a car accident hits her like a truck. The shaking hands, the clumsiness? Nooooo. It was just fatigue? Wasn't it? A brain biopsy? Shit!

Apparently, these two doctors were the best neurosurgeons in the best private hospital in the Midwest. But a brain biopsy?

Even Faith knew that a brain biopsy was a serious operation. A serious operation just to get more data was very... serious.

They would not have dared make the biopsy call frivolously. People with enough money to buy the hospital or sue it into bankruptcy were treated with kid gloves and charged for silk gloves.

The brain biopsy could well be just to cover their asses but something about the way the two had looked at each other suggested differently. Could there be something seriously wrong? No way. Fuck!

"Some cause happiness wherever they go; others, whenever they go." ~ Oscar Wilde

Chapter 9

From the semicircular Nurses' Station, Mandy watches Faith on the closed-circuit TV screen. Faith is distastefully holding a bedpan in one hand. Her other hand is heavily bandaged and is connected to a drip. Despite this, she repeatedly stabs the nurse alert button. The wobbling drip stand is tempted to topple over but seems reluctant to take a fall.

Faith stares up at the security camera in the corner. She is furious. "I know you can hear me! I will not piss in this… THING! You will carry me to the toilet so get some help! NOW!"

Nurse Mandy ducks involuntarily when the bedpan hurtles toward her on the screen. The muffled sound of a heavy metal object hitting a wall punctuates Faith's proclamation.

Wendy holds a patient file and watches a monitor where Faith's heart rate spikes. With a dour expression on her face, she comments. "No visitors. No wonder."

"And no next of kin either," chips in Mandy as she uses a remote to turn the volume down on Faith. "Well, at least she's getting stronger... Have they told her yet?"

"No one has the balls. They are rechecking the tests that they have already checked to see if there is a way out." Mandy shakes her head. They can both see a miserable Faith pouting petulantly on her bed. Mandy finally breaks the silence. "Yeah, I wouldn't wish that on anyone… not even her."

Later that day, during rounds, the Nurses' Station is temporarily unattended. A well-dressed man, carrying a bag and flowers, slips surreptitiously into Faith's private room.

Faith is resting her eyes when she senses a presence. It was early for lunch, but she was hungry. She opens her eyes and immediately regrets it. She is shocked and repulsed to see the last person in the world that she wanted to see standing smirking proudly at the foot of her bed.

Setting the bag down and moving surprisingly swiftly for a man who looked like he had swallowed a basketball, Chuck snatches up the nurse call button and holds it well beyond Faith's reach.

"Get out! GO. Now!" Faith shouts.

"Faith, you need to learn how to relax. I've come to bring a peace offering." Chuck chuckles and then flourishes the flowers that he has brought. He then places them upright at the foot of Faith's bed. Faith looks longingly at the nurse call button, but she knows that she cannot reach it.

It takes no great leap of intellect to tell what Faith is thinking. Even Chuck can make that jump. He goads Faith by dangling the button in front of her, just within her grasp. When she tries to snatch it, he yanks it back, laughing. He could do this all day, but security would probably have other ideas.

"Chucky… really? Recess must be over. You'll be missed soon."

Chuck plays his game once more; only this time when Faith snatches for it he allows her to grasp it but then he pulls the other end of the cable out of the wall. "Oops… sorry." Chuck casually wipes his sweaty brow with a towel before he throws it over the lens of the closed-circuit TV camera.

"Nurse! NURSE!"

Chuck moves to the side of Faith's bed and speaks softly. "I've had quite a week, Faith. Very stressful. Thanks to you – my reputation is in tatters, and I also lost most of my money. You made me very, very, very angry."

Chuck starts to stroke Faith's drip tube as he is talking. He accentuates each use of the word 'very' by tugging on the cannula hard enough to pull on the needle embedded in her vein. It hurts, but Faith doesn't make a sound. Tendrils of fear are starting to tingle up her spine. Chuck was always a few cards short of a full deck, but even for him, this was bizarre, psychopathic.

"I didn't think I could hate you any more than I already did, but…" Chuck strokes the drip bag. "Anyway, it all turned around

when I got your news, and... well, thanks for cheering me up."
Chuck's smile is sinister, obscene.

"Fire! Fire! F-I-R-E!"

"Oh please, Faith, how ungallant. Surely you can give me a moment to savor my victory... the nurses won't be back for a while, so you can save your breath, or not. Bernhard told me something funny yesterday when he gave me his job. I laughed. I really did when he told me... he explained how he orchestrated 'Faith's Folly,' all of it. He set you up, honey. Funny, eah?"

Faith is shocked, speechless. Was it possible? No. No. No. None of this could be happening. This was madness, delirium. She had stayed with Napoleon Brothers because... because Bernhard had...

Chuck runs his hand down the drip tube again. "Tell me, how does this thing work in veins filled with ice?" Chuck pauses, immensely proud. He had thought of that one himself. The power he had over Faith at this moment was intoxicating. "But enough chitchat. I just wanted to see you, you know, before you lose your mind... completely."

It was obviously a big setup for a crushing finish, but Faith doesn't understand what he is talking about. Chuck is disappointed by the lack of reaction from his big punch line. It was a zinger and yet... no reaction whatsoever?

"You sick, gutless bastard, GET OUT!" His smugness was disturbing; her skin felt like it was trying to crawl off her body to get away.

Chuck giggles, "They haven't told you yet, have they?" Faith's reaction confirms his sudden insight "Oh, this is priceless!" Chuck's exuberance was worse than his smugness.

Faith screams, "Get Out! NURSE!" Chuck leans over and plucks something from his bag. "No Faith, I can't leave until I have given you your present. Since you can't have my balls or my father's, I thought you might appreciate an alternative form of testicular nourishment." Chuck tries to give Faith a dripping tray of calf's testicles.

Finally, Faith works out how to bring help. She rips the sensors from her chest. Her heart rate monitor goes flat, a loud warning sound can be heard from inside and outside the room. Help was coming.

"Poor Faith. Poor, poor Faith. Oh, oh, wait a minute, noooo... rich Faith. Very rich, billionaire Faith."

A Doctor and a big, strong male nurse burst into the room. They are surprised to see a flat-lining patient sitting up in bed screaming at them.

"DOOR! OUT! GET HIM OUT NOW! GET HIM OUT! **NOW**!" The male nurse advances on Chuck who backs towards the door as another nurse comes rushing in. The heart rate monitor is switched off.

As Chuck reverses out of the room he gets the last words. "All that money ... but no life left to enjoy it. What a pity you can't take any of it with you when you die."

The door swings shut, and Chuck is gone but his final parting words stay with Faith. She starts to tremble uncontrollably, and the Doctor quickly prepares a sedative. With the needle comes blessed, but temporary, release.

"Anger is an acid that can do more harm to the vessel in which it is stored than to anything on which it is poured." ~ Mark Twain

Chapter 10

Faith had been running from herself for a long time. She was scathing of anyone seeking psychiatric help. Faith had never got into drugs, and she had never found comfort in the arms of alcohol either. She knew all too well how destructive alcohol could be.

Work was Faith's substance of choice and making money had become addictive and all-consuming. Even when she wasn't working, she was thinking of the markets, reading, researching. Long hours and constant busyness had been a recipe for financial success, if not happiness. Well, definitely not happiness but when you have no time to think about being happy then you don't miss it either.

Even after sleeping for 14 drug-assisted hours, Faith is still in shock from the poisonous vitriol of Chuck's surprise visit. The hospital was in serious damage control over the incident. Faith was sending a tsunami of manure their way.

The Doctors finally told her what they had been hoping to avoid. It wasn't just cowardice on their part, this variant of the disease had never been detected in the US before and it was a death sentence, so caution was warranted. Tests had been run several times on the first brain biopsy, but the results had not changed.

Faith had achieved another first. She was the first American to contract new variant Creutzfeldt - Jakob disease, sometimes called 'human mad cow' disease. It appeared that Faith had contracted it as a fatal legacy of a high British beef diet during a year-long trading stint in London. Fuck it! What else did you eat in London if you didn't like Indian food? What idiot thought that feeding ground-up bits of diseased cows to other unsuspecting cows was a good idea? Efficiency, economics, assholes.

Faith sits firmly on the throne of denial; this couldn't be happening, not to her. Despite all the evidence, she hopes against hope that this was all just a big, crazy mistake. Additional brain scans have been performed. The biopsy tissue had had a DNA check so they could definitively rule out the possibility of any lab mix-up.

Unfortunately, what was distressing her was that her gut was telling her that the disease prognosis fit with what she had been experiencing. Her hope was of a very low quality. At the moment, all Faith could feel was vulnerable, a feeling she had done everything in her considerable powers to avoid for a very long time.

Partnering with denial was a profound sadness crashing over Faith. She was helpless and there was no work that she could distract herself with. Even if Jesus popped in and cured her tomorrow; she would never go back to trading or the open toilet that was Napoleon Brothers.

Why? Why? Faith had been going through her long night of the soul since the early afternoon. It is late and she is exhausted. She has no answers.

An older nurse changes the drip bag and puts fresh bandages on her arm. Faith looks terrible, pasty, sad, and teary. All the fight is gone, replaced with self-pity. "Why do you even bother?" she asks. The nurse gently finishes dressing her arm before answering. "I do what I can."

"No one will care, no lover, no child, no one... just an ungrateful cat."

The nurse checks the circulation in Faith's fingers, to make sure that the bandages are not too tight. She holds the hand for a moment and gives it a gentle squeeze. Faith squeezes back; she wants to keep holding the nurse's warm, soft hand but she lets it go.

"I care, people care... if you let them." The nurse opens the tap on the drip. "This will help you sleep."

Faith speaks so softly that the nurse is not sure if she is talking to her or not. "I just wanted enough so I never had to worry about it and then..." Faith yawns. "I'm just so tired... I just... I can't fight this; it's my own body... I'm just so tired... so... tired." Faith slips into sleep, into blackness until...

Faith is sitting in a well-lit, oak-paneled courtroom. She is jerked forcefully to her feet as the Judge enters the room. After the Judge takes his seat, Faith is pushed down into her chair. The Judge leans back and puts his polished cowboy boots slowly up on his desk. He pulls a thick cigar from an inside pocket and lights it. The 'No Smoking' signs were decorative, not instructive. The Judge is Bernhard. The wig suits him. The power he is used to.

Faith is on trial; she is also handcuffed. The handcuffs are extremely heavy. Faith knows what they are made of before she even examines them, they are made of gold.

A side door opens, and the jurors walk in and take their seats. They are all different shapes and sizes, and all dressed like they were on their way to a night of boot scootin.' Looking at them made Faith want to vomit.

They all sported the smirking face of Chuck Jones, even the five women. The Chuck who is the head juror stands up and walks a folded slip of paper up to Judge Bernhard. As he hands it over, they whisper together and share what must be a funny joke. Head Chuck turns around and stares at Faith. He rubs his forehead with his middle finger.

As if on cue, all the other jurors rub their foreheads with their middle fingers too. Bernhard takes his boots down from the desk one boot at a time and opens the slip of paper. He starts to laugh. He laughs so hard that he hits the gavel several times just to add to his mirth rather than trying to halt it. When he finally stops laughing there is silence.

"This court finds Faith McCormack guilty of wasting her life and awards her entire fortune to someone much more deserving, Mr. Chuck Jones. Congratulations Chuck, eah?"

The prosecutor, who also happens to be a Chuck, takes a bow. He then shuffles over to Faith and sneers, "Even if you could take it, you won't need it where you are going."

Faith becomes incensed, this was so unfair. She strains at the handcuffs. She would claw the face right off her taunting Chuck if only she could get her hands free.

Faith screams, "You bastards, you lying, cheating bastards. I'll show you, fuck you. I will take it all with me, all of it! ALL OF IT! Do you hear me? Every last shekel!"

*"It's not denial. I'm just selective about the reality
I accept." ~ Bill Watterson*

Chapter 11

Faith is drenched in sweat. She is thrashing about, arms flailing. Everything is blurry again; she is trapped in a horrific nightmare. Her pulse spikes which triggers the heart rate monitor's strident alarm.

"Nooo! NOOO! This is not the way it's supposed to be!"

A security guard forcefully pushes the door open to see what is going on. A nurse rushes in behind him. Faith's drip line has torn out and a crimson stain now decorates her bandage.

The nurse beckons to the guard to help her restrain Faith. She quickly injects Faith with a sedative.

In the corridor outside Faith's room, oblivious to the pandemonium nearby, a Tibetan nun is walking peacefully past.

The drugs are kicking in and for Faith, the world has shifted to slow motion. The nun fades in and out of focus. The maroon robes over the nun's yellow shirt are the only colors that Faith can see. The robe swishes back and forth hypnotically.

Another nurse rushes into the room. She grabs an oxygen mask to put over Faith's face. Faith tries to get a better view of the door.

The nun turns to look at the commotion but the nurse steps in front of Faith and pushes her down on the bed. When the nurse finally moves the nun is gone. Was it real?

Over the next few days, Faith retreats into herself and onto online research: nvCJD or new variant Creutzfeldt - Jakob disease.

Her hospital bed is transformed into a bed desk. Three monitors have been set up around her. She sleeps little. Unfortunately, there is no good news.

An exasperated Dr. Kleinstein is standing next to Faith's bed. He is in a tizz. "Before I gave you my opinion on your condition, I studied all the test results thoroughly and consulted widely with colleagues. As a professional, I encouraged you to get a second opinion."

Kleinstein continues his lecture, "Madam, at times, if the first two opinions are not in accord, then a third opinion is prudent. Yes. But, when the first four opinions are all in precise alignment, why do you insist on flying in another specialist? And this, this Cambridge upstart? I told you that he is not well regarded..." The door opens and a weak-chinned, be-tweeded weasel man, who looks to be in his mid-thirties enters the room.

"Ahh, Professor Irving how nice to meet you," effuses Dr. Kleinstein.

Professor Irving has flown a long way for this meeting. After he is introduced, he checks Faith's chart, excuses himself, and confers briefly with Dr. Kleinstein.

He approaches Faith's bed. In a very serious and superficially concerned tone, he says. "Madam, unfortunately in your case, as you know, the damage to your brain has already occurred and the symptoms of this damage can no longer be ignored. There is a little good news. It is not contagious and fortunately, it has been detected earlier than in most cases for which much credit must go to Dr. Kleinstein." Dr. Kleinstein purrs from each side of his two faces.

"Regrettably, all I can tell you is what you have already been told. The medical evidence is beyond dispute. You have a rare form of human "mad cow" disease. There is no cure, indeed even the mechanism for it is still not well understood and I am sorry... it is invariably fatal."

"I thought perhaps that some of the innovative treatments for dementia that we are experimenting with might help. But sadly, whilst we could enroll you in our program, the treatments will make no positive difference to your condition, and the side effects could be detrimental."

Faith had hoped that some of his new experiments might have helped. She was not the kind of person who just listened to experts and then swallowed. She was a spitter and this pumped-up asshole had given her false hope. Why had he even bothered to fly out? After a decent pause, the young Professor continues.

"Of course, much of the difficulty with nvCJD is that, because it is so rare, not much research has been done. Ms. McCormack, I believe that with the resources I have available and sufficient funding we might well be able to come up with a treatment in several years' time."

He pauses to gauge Faith's reaction to his opening pitch for a large chunk of a dying woman's estate. Professor Irving was one of the youngest Professors in Cambridge's medical community. Some described him as bold. Other people used all capital letters and different words.

Faith stares at Irving. The silence continues until he becomes uneasy. His collar is suddenly too tight. Finally, Faith launches at him. "You pompous prick. I don't have that long, and you know that."

"Well, umm... no, definitely not," he huffs. "It is possible, but highly unlikely, that you would benefit from any research, BUT at least you would know that any bequest you make might help future sufferers of Creutzfeldt-Jakob..."

Faith looks at her bodyguard, Chad, who is standing just inside the door. Faith had asked for a large man, without a neck, who could kill with his hands. She hoped that Chuck would be stupid enough to try and visit again.

Faith silences Irving with one word. "Door!"

Chad quickly moves his considerable bulk between Faith and Professor Irving. He also says, "door" but when he says it, he adds the promise of physical harm if he is not obeyed instantly.

Faith shakes her head grimly as Irving scuttles away. Dr. Kleinstein is equal parts alarmed and pleased so he says nothing.

Irving, trying to extract his tail from between his legs, bumps into Faith's lawyer, David Struder as he tries to enter the room. Chad stops the lawyer at the doorway with a firm, very large hand to David's chest. Chad looks at Faith who gives a nod of approval. A disappointed Chad steps aside.

David looks curiously at Chad and winks cheekily at him before he walks over and pulls up a chair next to Faith's bed. David is middle-aged, square-jawed, and ruggedly handsome. He exudes competence and confidence.

"Sorry I couldn't get here sooner." He strokes his thick black beard. "Only got back from the South American jungle yesterday. So, maybe now you'll ditch that red 'toy' and buy the safer Mercedes I ..."

David stops talking as he looks at Faith. She looks like hell. He had never seen her this way. It dawns on him that perhaps there is more going on than just the aftereffects of a car crash. He looks from Faith across to Chad, then over to Dr. Kleinstein who shakes his head. Finally, he looks back to Faith who manages a very weak grin. He starts again but the bonhomie is gone.

"I ... um... Faith, are you OK? I mean apart from, you know, being knocked around?"

Faith looks at Dr. Kleinstein and Chad and nods toward the door. This leaves David alone with Faith.

"David... Well, David... I'm... there's no other way to say it. Shit! David, I'm dying." It shocked Faith to hear herself say it, it made it sound real. Fuck!

David watches the emotions race across her face. "No, No. You can't be... No?"

Faith tries to avoid being melodramatic. She disliked soap operas so much that she avoided bubble baths. She was not a sudsy type of person.

"Really, I am. I have been diagnosed with new variant Creutzfeldt - Jakob disease, an extremely rare but I am assured a 100% fatal, incurable, even untreatable, disease. It probably caused the car accident and would also explain my... dark moods of late. I was put into an induced coma following the accident and there were some anomalies in the electroencephalograph test results. I am *really* lucky that they detected it so early."

Faith doesn't sound very lucky; she sounds sharply sarcastic. She tries very hard to keep her voice even, as if she was merely recounting the details of a trade that had gone wrong.

David is stunned into silence. "No? How?" and after a pause, "Surely not."

Faith nails David with an intense stare. He was not helping her. Talking about it was much harder than she had thought it would be. David progresses from stunned to shocked.

"David, I have thought about this a great deal." Faith pauses because what she is about to say deserves a decent space before delivery which is quite different from melodrama for melodrama's sake.

"David, I have decided that I want to take my entire fortune with me when I die, everything, every last nickel. As my lawyer, your job is to find me a way to do that."

"Look Faith with your... clout I'm sure we can find a cure. I can help you beat this. I have a friend..."

"David!" Faith says this more sharply than she had meant to. "Whilst you have been running naked in the jungle or whatever, I have been dealing with this, talking to experts and doing my own research because you know how much I trust 'experts.' Don't you think I have already explored every possibility? Every remote chance to beat it? Every hope?"

Faith takes a deep breath and sighs. "There is no cure. New variant Creutzfeldt - Jakob disease is a type of spongiform encephalopathy. Some of my brain tissue has tiny holes in it giving it a sponge-like texture that is not reversible. The damage has been happening for years. Ever since I ate beef contaminated with mad cow disease. Even the witch doctors don't offer miracle cures for what I have."

David's jaw drops. He is in utter disbelief, and he can't look at Faith.

"David, did you hear what I said?"

"Phew, umm, yeah... I'm just in a bit of shock, which probably makes two of us." David stands up and starts pacing. He was a pacer. He did his best thinking when he was pacing. "You want to leave everything. OK ... Who do you want to leave it to? Starving children, orphans, African Aids programs, NRDC, Sea Shepherd? Rainforest rescue in South America or Indonesia? ..."

"Shut up and listen! I'm going to say this slowly, not because you are stupid but because you are having trouble listening. I don't want to leave anything behind; I don't owe anybody anything. I will take everything with me when I die, everything. Your job is to find me a way to do that."

David has a new appreciation for the word dumbfounded. He is incapable of speech, hence the dumb part of the word but he was floundering rather than founding. Perhaps a more accurate word would be dumbfloundered? In his dumbfloundered state, all he can do is stare at a brittle, bristling Faith.

"I think I'm missing something here, again. I'm trying but I really don't understand. I mean, obviously, you can't take everything with you."

David hopes desperately that this is all a very bizarre, practical joke. Unlikely or, better still, maybe he hadn't woken up from the Ayahuasca yet? In a jesting tone, David continues, "I mean you just can't. Unless you want to be buried in a solid diamond coffin inside a designer pyramid or maybe in a nice sphinx... perhaps?"

David trails off as the audience was clearly not going with him. Working for Faith was often a tough gig but this time...

44

"No, No, NO, No! NO. No! Look, I don't know how to do it, that's why I called you." Faith stops to gather her thoughts.

"I know I'm dying before my time, before I have had time to enjoy the wealth I have worked so hard for. This is monstrously unfair. I was about to retire, really retire... David, I need to go on, somehow, and if you are not interested in helping, then I will find someone who is."

David had inhaled in readiness to deliver his rebuttal but as Faith's words sink in, he stops and lets all the air out at once. This was his client; there would not be a, 'someone who is,' someone who didn't even know Faith. He pauses and shakes his head trying desperately to clear it. There was a tight ball of fear in the pit of his stomach, but he had to try to talk reason to her. He wasn't just Faith's lawyer, he considered himself Faith's friend though he had no idea if she thought the same way.

"Faith... look, you're very emotional, not rational." The cobra coils, ready to strike. David adds hastily, "Quite understandably. Now, I'm not a psychiatrist, but this sounds like a form of denial to me."

Faith stays coiled but says nothing. David is incredulous. He knows that he just lit a fuse and that if he didn't put it out soon, there would be an almighty explosion. He suddenly felt like Wile E. Coyote. Did that make Faith the Road Runner? At least he was in a hospital.

Cautiously, David continues. "Faith, even you can't take any of it with you when you die. It is the only universal truth left. Everybody knows that."

As Faith becomes hysterical, she temporarily suspends her dislike of melodrama and... KABOOM! "Well, David, I don't know that and neither do you because neither of us has fucking died before! I have worked so hard. So HARD. I haven't had a life. I earned my wealth and I want to enjoy it! I want to enjoy it... finally! DO YOU HEAR ME?"

David's ears were ringing. Yes, he had heard her, half of the hospital had heard her, but what was she asking? Come on, really? But now that the explosives were gone, maybe there was a chance for reason.

"Faith, Faith it's impossible. Even you can't bribe the ferryman."

"If you don't want to help me fine, go fuck yourself, but do this for me and you can name your price."

The buzzing in David's ears suddenly changes tone and all he can hear is the sound of an old-fashioned cash register ringing up a sale. It helps clear David's head. OK, what Faith was asking was impossible BUT she wanted his help. She wanted his help enough that he could name his price, but not enough that she wouldn't replace him with someone else. And, if she replaced him, she would probably find some complete con lawyer to prey on her newfound vulnerability. Faith was great at making money, but her people skills were... well, they were shit.

Name your price? This was business now but how much to ask for? David tries to do some mental arithmetic, but his brain seems to be frozen. Think! Think! ... Got it! Shrewdly he looks up at Faith.

"The Picasso?"

Faith gasps. The Picasso? Sure, the Picasso had initially been a way of diversifying her investments and it was showing a 200% profit over three years, but she had come to, she was... well, she was quite attached to it. Most people would have used the 'L' word, 'love', but quite attached was as far as Faith would allow herself to go with paint.

Whilst Faith had threatened to find someone else, she really wanted David to help her. He was hired help, but he had been her advisor from the early days, and she trusted him. He was the closest thing to a friend that she had. Was she ever more than just a client to him? Faith sighs.

"The Picasso."

*"Death is not the greatest loss in life. The greatest
loss is what dies inside us while we live."* ~
Norman Cousins

Chapter 12

Faith is relieved to finally be out of hospital. The hospital
had not wanted to discharge her. Of course they didn't, but the
reluctance to discharge was based on financial grounds, not
medical. The 'Sacred Wallet' hospital, as Faith called it, was
making a lot of money keeping Faith a pin cushion and she had had
enough.

Sore in body and in mind, Faith is struggling to come to
terms with her diagnosis. It didn't seem real. Of course, she had
read about people suddenly being diagnosed with a fatal disease,
but she never thought it could happen to her. Those things were
only supposed to happen to other people.

At times she would be furious, angry at everything, which
was one way of dealing with it, but the problem was that Faith had
trouble releasing her anger in an appropriate way. Regularly
shouting at the hospital staff had helped and she had also broken a
few bits and vases at the hospital which she was not proud of.
Despite these outbursts, the anger was still there, simmering away
like a drum of rice on a large stove with the lid on. As soon as you
look away, it explodes and makes a horrible and sticky but gluten-
free mess.

Faith spent decades learning how to suppress her emotions,
particularly fear. In trading, if you gave in to fear you found
yourself running in a close-pressed pack of panicking lemmings.
Do lemmings panic? Or were they just stupid? Faith is pretty sure

that when the idiot lemming behind you 'accidentally' bumped you off the cliff that that would induce panic. Whatever. Run scared in the market and you end up losing both your financial and emotional capital.

Faith's gut feelings were something different, they were instinct, and she had learned through harsh lessons how to listen to those.

Faith strokes Fluffy as she sits in a plush leather chair watching David pace nervously. His bulging briefcase is closed on the couch. He clears his throat. He clears his throat again and glances up at the Picasso on the wall, a masterpiece. His hands break out in a sweat. He has to tear his gaze away.

"Well, basically, um… initially we have come up with three possible choices, but I think you'll only be interested in the first one." David pauses for dramatic effect. It is effort that is wasted on his audience. Moving on quickly before the dramatic void is filled by him looking foolish, he proclaims, "Cryonics."

Faith involuntarily shivers at the mention of cryonics as David reverently removes a thick blue leather folder from his briefcase. Fluffy jumps down off Faith's lap and begins to rub herself against David's legs.

"David? We live in Chicago! Just look outside. Imagine a never-ending Chicago winter until they can finally thaw you out? If they EVER thaw you out? If the cleaner doesn't accidentally kick the power cord…"

"Oh, Faith, that is so unfair. That Far Side cartoon is a comic, a jape, a joke, one that the cryonics industry has strongly objected to. It can hardly be a valid reason to not even consider this as an option. It is a very good option."

Faith shivers again, "Cryonics? Really?" The 'really' was not an invitation to further inquiry. David is appalled at Faith's attitude. She didn't even want to consider it. Fluffy was also starting to annoy him. Cats? Really?

"Oh, come on Faith. At least hear me out. Obviously, you will feel nothing. The technology today is brilliant, cryopreservation of the whole body at temperatures of 77 degrees Kelvin. They use cryoprotectants to replace water inside cells with chemicals that prevent the cells from being damaged by low temperatures. There is a clinic in Switzerland that has indicated that with your diagnosis they are open to the possibility of starting the process even before you are pronounced clinically dead, and they won't revive you until there is a cure for nvCJD. Full cost estimates are included. Here, have a look at these photos…"

There is no response from Faith. David tries to hand her the folder, but she refuses to even touch it. He holds the folder out again, unsuccessfully.

"Faith, just consider it, OK? You want to go on? This is a scientific way to achieve that goal."

Faith looks up at David but does not move to take the eagerly proffered folder. Faith did not have to argue, for her it was a non-choice, simple, perhaps not totally logical, but simple.

Disappointed and not hiding it, David whacks the folder onto the table. It makes a satisfyingly loud slap. He shoos Fluffy away from his leg. Damn cat. Double damn, cat and cat hair. His lucky suit would need dry cleaning after this or throwing out.

David removes a gold-colored leather folder out of his briefcase along with a dose of sarcasm. "OK, good, that will save us an hour or three. Moving right along, Option 2, perhaps a little more controversial… cloning." This time David ignores drama and goes for terse, which he nails.

David looks at Faith who is impassive. No reaction. Nada. Blast!

Both of these options were highly predictable, and Faith had already considered and discarded them. At least with this one, Faith humors David by taking the folder. She flicks through it, without interest.

"The technology isn't quite there yet but the best possibility for the future is to harvest eggs from your ovaries and ..."

Faith shakes her head which stops David mid-pitch. What now? Faith looks like she has just sucked on a lemon. "All my eggs were poached a long time ago."

"You're sure?"

The question does not warrant a response. Faith stares at David and he turns away, blushing.

"Right, right, well, of course, you'd know, wouldn't you?" With that, David sighs and takes out the last folder from his briefcase. It is pink. It even has a pink ribbon on it. His shoulders sag as he throws it to the floor.

"Well with cloning now they can harvest other cells from your body, preserve them, and then use them to create a clone when that technology has advanced somewhat..."

Faith is still leafing through the folder. David can't help it; he keeps looking over her shoulder at the Picasso. Faith shudders, she's just sucked on that damn lemon again.

"David, part of me loves the idea of cloning, and a bigger part of me is repulsed by the idea. I don't know, it's creepy, creating Faithenstein. A lump of flesh that looks like me ... but how could a clone be me? It won't have my memories; the bad, the bad, and the... not so bad. It will be a collection of cells with my DNA but how could it be me?"

"I don't know, Faith. Nobody knows, but then, after throwing out cryonics and with the other one," he points to the pink folder, "not being viable... you really don't have too many choices left besides being buried in a pyramid... do you?"

Faith bristles at David's comment. "For Picasso, David! We are talking about Picasso, a piece that is considered to be his *magnum opus*. These, David, these..." Faith indicates the folders including the one in her hand.

"These are shite, not masterpiece, more like kindergarten finger painting. Fluffy could have done better and, what's worse, you have wasted my time which is more precious than ever."

Faith hands the bullion-colored folder back. David tries to swap it for the cryonics folder, but Faith won't even look at the blue folder.

"Christ, Faith! You won't even consider the only scientific possibilities that are open to you." David could feel the Picasso slipping from his grasp. He had the perfect place to hang it in his house. He had already had new lighting and security installed.

"Well, Jesus, David! Maybe when you're dying, you'll understand why I am so 'picky.' My gut is repulsed by the options, none are right for me. End of story."

"Normal people leave things to their loved ones... why don't you just leave it all to..." In his anger and frustration, David realizes that he has skated onto very thin ice. Did Faith have any loved ones? Besides herself? Improvising quickly, he makes a desperate jump for safe ground and points to... "Fluffy?"

Faith strokes Fluffy and is rewarded with a loud purr. The ice shatters behind him but David is safe, for now. Fluffy stares at him with her two different-colored eyes. David was always highly disconcerted by Faith's cat. He had carelessly called Fluffy's eyes freaky once and Faith had aggressively handed him his ass in a basket. It had seemed a huge overreaction for a throwaway comment, but David had never criticized Fluffy since.

"Call me 'abnormal' then, David, but leaving everything to Fluffy would be totally pathetic." Faith changes her tone. With great affection, she says, "No offense Fluffy." Fluffy continues to purr, no offense taken. Faith gently picks Fluffy up and places her on the couch. She moves over to stand next to the Picasso.

Fluffy leaps lightly onto David's briefcase just as her anus needs a thorough licking. Her leg immediately goes over her head and her pink tongue... well...

David has not been watching Fluffy though; he has been watching Faith closely. She points to the painting. "Look at this, David."

David does, he has hardly stopped looking at it. It invokes an indescribable yearning in him which was much more than the multi-million-dollar value. It was truly one of a kind.

"You named your price and we both know you went high, very, very high. Did you think that it would be easy? Grow up, David! For this, you can find a way." Faith is being harsh, but that crap in colored folders? Please.

David stands up and straightens his tie. He runs his hands through his carefully coiffured hair, something he rarely did. He is disappointed, frustrated. Yes, he thought he and his staff had found an easy way. Because they could not find any other alternatives and just maybe, David thought, maybe the Picasso was a thank you for all of his years of loyal service and his advice that had paid for the painting a hundred times over and now? Now the cat was licking itself on his best briefcase. Fuck it!

"Well, Faith, as your lawyer, my learned advice is this... reincarnate as a cat next lifetime then you can sit around and lick your own ass all day instead of paying people to do it for you!"

Deep furrows crease Faith's forehead. Ouch! She had thick skin but that hurt coming from David. She was having trouble controlling her shaking and couldn't hide it. A shit day was turning to diarrhea. For the first time, she felt trapped by her circumstances. Up to now, in her life, she had always at least pretended that she had choices, even if at one time she had chosen suicide.

David sneezes and then forcefully shoos Fluffy off his briefcase. David was definitely a 'big dog' guy. He didn't see the purpose of domesticated cats, they were his pet hate, pun intended. His wife had bought him the book '101 Uses for a Dead Cat.' He loved it. Being allergic to cats certainly didn't help him find affection for felines but it did seem to make him popular with the creatures.

David snatches up his valise. He brushes the disgusting cat hair off it and stomps towards the door without looking back. Fluffy instantly does the crazy cat thing. She starts by making a mighty leap from the couch to the bookshelf. Fluffy then literally flies around the room, zigzagging and jumping about as if she had just swallowed a whole hive of bees. Books and knick knacks are knocked off the bookcase. An antique bone China cup becomes a casualty as it shatters on the floor.

There is a loud SLAM as David exits the penthouse and as abruptly as it started, Fluffy stops, stretches, and then curls up in her basket as if nothing had happened. Cats. Even Faith is surprised. Fluffy was an inherently lazy cat and that performance had been highly active, almost aerobic. What had gotten into her?

Faith walks over to the scattered books. Fluffy has fallen asleep. Several books have fallen but the book on top of the pile is an expensive coffee table book, '*TIBET: THE ROOF OF THE WORLD BETWEEN PAST AND PRESENT.*' It has fallen open to a page dominated by a photo of His Holiness, the 14th Dalai Lama.

Faith picks it up and studies the photo. On the opposite page is a photo of Lhamo Latso, the caption reads "the sacred lake where Regent Reting had the vision which led to the discovery of the reincarnation of the 14th Dalai Lama."

Faith sits down on the couch with the book and begins to flip through it. "Thank you, Fluffy." There would be fresh salmon in her dish tonight.

"I may not have gone where I intended to go, but I think I have ended up where I needed to be." ~
Douglas Adams

Chapter 13

The Army base looks even fouler in daylight than it did at night. To Tibetans, it is a discordant abomination that is out of place in Lhasa. Unfortunately, the more the Chinese authorities replaced old Tibetan houses with concrete apartment boxes, the more it was starting to blend in.

An angry PLA Officer leafs savagely through a passport. He checks the front again. DAMN! It is still a US Passport. He opens it to the back and takes out the piece of paper which has a unique watermark, the watermark of a United States Senator.

The influential Senator from Illinois had written a letter personally endorsing the Tibetan study trip by the bruised and battered person who is standing, with the help of two of his soldiers, right in front of him. A photo of the Dalai Lama falls out of the passport.

The Officer stands up and looks Tenzin in the eye. He rips up the photo and slams the passport loudly onto the desk, bending it. He shouts at the soldiers in the room. He then shouts some more which makes him feel better, but the soldiers? Not so good. They knew this Officer was more bite than bark. When he barked, bad things happened to people. He shouts at Tenzin in Chinese, sharing his frothing spittle freely.

Tenzin pretends that she does not understand a word. Whilst hardly fluent, Tenzin catches enough to get the gist of what the

Officer is spraying. He is furious that the soldiers had not found the passport when they caught her AND they should have been more careful when they were beating her. So many marks and cuts. He calls them stupid several different ways and threatens to report them to the regional commander. There were many postings worse than Lhasa and he promises to find one for them.

Carefully he folds up the letter from the Senator and replaces it in the creased passport. He aches to beat Tenzin himself. He misses the old days. Instead, he gestures with his arms and shouts even louder for the soldiers to get the American filth out of his office. He orders them to clean her up and give her some food. Tenzin does not react, but inwardly she sighs, they never bothered to clean or feed corpses.

The soldiers grab Tenzin roughly and shove her out the door. The Officer keeps the passport. He looks at the letter again and sits down. Nervously, he picks up the telephone, but he slams it quickly back into the receiver. A lesser phone would have broken. Finally, after composing himself as best he can, he dials a number. It is cold but he has started to perspire, and no amount of licking can keep his lips moist.

As Tenzin is frog-marched away, she looks up and sees the magnificent Potala Palace perched on Marpo Ri Hill overlooking Lhasa. The magnificent 13 story 'White Palace' had been the home of the Dalai Lamas since the 7th century; well from the 7th century until 1959 when Tenzin Gyatso fled for his life from his beloved country.

The clouds part and the Potala Palace is suddenly bathed in bright sunshine. After being isolated in a dark cell, it is blinding but Tenzin does not try to shield her eyes from the glare. It was likely the last time she would ever see it and she greedily drinks in every part of the sprawling structure, trying to mentally block out the 'modern' atrocities on the sides of the hill.

Faith is also looking at the Potala Palace, but the surrounding environment is different. The beautiful landscape photo in the book was taken before the redevelopment of Lhasa. She reads that UNESCO added the unique Potala Palace to its World Heritage List in 1994 in an attempt to stop, or at least delay, the throwing up of concrete apartment blocks around it.

Faith's phone rings. She picks it up out of habit, but her head is 7,500 miles away. She continues to read: "The Palace had over 1,000 rooms, 10,000 shrines, and 200,000 statues. The sloping walls average 3m thick and 5m thick at the base. During construction, copper was poured into the foundations to help protect it from earthquakes…"

David is using the hands-free phone system in his Mercedes to talk while he drives. He is feeling terrible about the way he left Faith. "Faith? Hi, look it's me, David. I just want to say sorry about before. I was way out of line... I had Picasso fever, no excuse, I know…"

Faith has the ability to interrupt even when she is distracted. "David, stop. It's forgotten… almost forgotten. I have to ask you something. Do you believe in reincarnation?"

There is a brief pause before David responds. "Well, it was Voltaire who said, "it is no more surprising to be born twice than it is to be born once."

"David, do lawyers ever give a straight answer? Do you? Do you David, not do you Voltaire, do you believe in reincarnation?"

"Um... Yeah, actually I do."

"Hmmm, surprisingly, me too but I've never really thought about it until a few minutes ago. Thank you again, Fluffy."

"Faith? Hello? You still there?"

Faith is now looking at a gaggle of young Tibetan Buddhist monks standing together smiling. It appears that they had been engaged in horseplay just a moment before the snap. The warmth and a certain cheekiness in their smiles have been captured by the photographer. Even Faith can't help smiling as she looks at it.

"David, I need you to prepare a different colored folder for me, a saffron-colored one, with yellow trimming... How much do you know about Tibetan Buddhism?"

After finishing her conversation with a relieved, confused, and worried David, Faith continues to flip the book. She opens it at the very front and notices some bold black handwriting on the inside cover.

'Dear Faith, Happy Birthday! This book has photos of some of the most beautiful and remote places on Earth. Reminded me of you. Love, David. P.S. I bet you $50.00 you never even open this book.'

The date was from several years earlier. Back when David was doing a lot of work for Faith on different company structures and negotiating Faith's investments in some early startup technology companies.

Most of the startups had failed but a few had been spectacularly profitable, hundreds of millions of dollars spectacularly profitable. It had been a very busy time, but then when hadn't it been?

Faith didn't remember opening this present. She may not have. Faith's housekeeper sometimes did that for her when she was snowed under with gratuities. Brokerage houses, banks, and general brownnosers regularly sent presents. This one had got lost in the mix.

Regret pays a visit, and Faith puts her head in her hands after she rereads the note from David.

"There is no need for temples, no need for complicated philosophies. My brain and my heart are my temples; my philosophy is kindness." ~ His Holiness the 14th Dalai Lama

Chapter 14

Faith is sitting in a comfortable leather chair in David's spacious office. She is happy to be out and about for a change. The trading screens in her penthouse had yet to be removed and she found them distracting. Her trading instincts were constantly getting piqued. They would be gone by the time she got home.

A maroon leather folder is open on her lap. David had a very good leather supplier; the guy or gal was a real craftsperson. Her coffee is half drunk. David has dark bags under his eyes; he is visibly exhausted and a little bit shaky. He and his team of researchers had been hard-lining coffee all night and not that weak, watery, homeopathic, dripolator rubbish.

David refused to support the drug cartels by using cocaine, so he bought an Italian-made espresso machine for the office. Everyone in his company had been barista trained so they could make an excellent cup of coffee. Good coffee was just not good enough in the Struder and Associates law practice.

David was a self-confessed coffee snob, but too much of a good thing with coffee could be a bad thing, time for another detox. He could already feel the coffee withdrawal headache on its way.

A smooth black stone statue of Buddha sits on one of the shelves behind his desk, next to a photo of David with his wife and two young children. The kids look to be two or five years old to Faith but then Faith had very little idea in these matters. Faith had forgotten that David had a family. After taking a sip of her coffee, which was superb, she continues their conversation on reincarnation.

"David, what I remember is this. I never even met Geoff, this friend of my older brother. I heard about him a lot. I was single and interested, but we just kept missing each other. When I heard that Geoff had died in a car crash, I almost collapsed. It was very strange. I felt a profound sense of loss, more even than when my poor brother took his own life a few months later. Rationally, I can't explain it. I felt I knew Geoff, somehow... From previous lifetimes? How else? If only we'd met, connected ... things would be..."

Faith looks up at David's happy family snap. She sighs... "Would be different and then, of course, there is Chuck. I hated him the moment I saw him before he had even uttered one ignorant, arrogant, racist word. So, I've believed in reincarnation for a long time without believing in it, if you know what I mean. But I've never really thought about it. Got kind of... caught up."

What Faith is not saying in words is that she had made some poor choices, choosing work over relationships. Their eyes meet briefly and there is a moment of awkwardness. Faith looks down at the folder.

"So... um... in theory, if someone could actually find my reincarnation, would it be legally possible to leave everything to... to, well, to me?"

David had been expecting this question. "Definitely! Setting up a Faith II trust account is straightforward." Faith stands up and despite the discomfort and the shaking in her hand; she starts excitedly pacing the room.

"So... in fact, I can leave everything... to, to the person who did all the hard work! To me! To Future Faith! If you can make this work, you deserve Picasso." In her exhilaration, Faith actually hugs David, though she soon becomes self-conscious and awkwardly disengages.

David tries to sound casual. He had expected the question but is dreading the next part. "But, yeah, um, Faith... as pathetic as it is, do you know why people really leave their fortunes to their pets?"

"Because they hate people, but they love their cat?"

David shakes his head 'no' and then, reluctantly, 'yes.' "OK, sometimes that may be the case but the main reason, Faith, is because they can find them! Finding Fluffy after you die is easy. Food out, Fluffy found. Give the cat a fortune, easy! Finding an incarnation is, well, not the same, it is tricky, to say the least. There is no science behind it, no microchip, no computer program, and no map to follow."

Faith is extremely excited about this new possibility. She had pretty much stopped listening. "Sure, sure ... but if these Tibetans can find the... the... what do they call him?"

"The Dalai Lama?"

"Yeah, him, the Dullai Lamo, if they can find his reincarnation 12 times..."

David corrects her, "13 times."

"Better still, then I'm damn sure that, for the right price, they will find my reincarnation once, for starters." Faith's overwhelming confidence was not, in this case, infectious. David is fighting an inner struggle. He knew it was not as simple as that.

"I... you're, they may ... but it is highly unlikely. Look, these people are not guns for hire, they are not reincarnation mercenaries. Finding certain incarnations is a fundamental part of the Tibetan Buddhist religion. It is not a profit center."

Faith shrugs David's comment off. For a moment, her face screws up in pain. She is keeping it together, just. Finally, she had a solution she could focus on. The thought of leaving everything to herself, well her next self, was intoxicating.

"David, everyone has their price. I've paid my price and well, you're a lawyer... everyone has a price." David looks hurt by Faith's comment. Many lawyers had indeed given lawyers a bad name, but he was not like them, and to have Faith throw it in his face after everything he had done for her. He knew she was callous and self-centered but even so.

"Right, so you just tell me what you want, and I write the contracts. That's the way it's always been." Faith is dimly aware that she has offended David.

"David, I know this sounds absolutely crazy." David looks away from her. "Please do this for me... for old time's sake." Faith puts the book on Tibet on David's desk as she picks up her purse. "You can have this back, and... thank you, David."

Faith gives David an uneasy kiss on the cheek and opens the door, leaving David stunned.

The traffic is heavy on the way back to her apartment, but Faith doesn't notice. The limousine driver weaves his way through it with confidence. There is no need to hurry. Faith is reading the 'Tibetan Book of Living and Dying' by Sogyal Rinpoche. The driver has the radio on and Paul Kelly's song 'YOU CAN'T TAKE IT WITH YOU' comes on. Faith cranks up the volume.

Paul Kelly croons, "You might own a great big factory." Faith responds, "Check." "Oil wells on sacred land." Faith didn't know for certain, but she gives herself the benefit of the doubt. "Check, check." Paul Kelly, "You might be successful in real estate." "Check, check, check." "You could even be a football star." Faith feels her bosoms, "Pass." Paul Kelly bursts into the chorus... "But yooouuuu can't take it with yooouuuu. You can't take it with you, though you might pile it up hiiiigh…"

There is a steely glint in Faith's eyes as she says, "Just watch me!"

After Faith leaves, David sits heavily in his desk chair and spins idly back and forth and then forth and back. He is tired, very tired but his heart was beating so fast he was sure that if he had one more coffee it would jump out of his chest and dance on his desk.

He leans forward and picks up the book on Tibet. There is a paper clip on the first page holding a $50 bill. He unpins the money and finds that Faith has written, in big red writing under his scrawl, 'Dear David, it was my loss. Sorry. Faith XOXOXO.'

David flicks open the book and looks at the photos of the tree-covered mountains that surround Dharamsala, India. The book explains that Dharamsala is where the democratic Tibetan Government in Exile was established. After the 1959 Tibetan uprising, the Dalai Lama and tens of thousands of Tibetans fled the Chinese occupation. They set up various refugee settlements with the help of the Indian Government. It was a very difficult time for the Tibetan refugees who were acclimated to the high altitude of the Tibetan plateau, many succumbed to tropical diseases and heat exhaustion. Dharamsala, situated in the upper reaches of the Kangra Valley at an elevation of 1,457m, has a more hospitable climate than many of the lower refugee settlements.

Chuck Jones had privately been promised Bernhard's job by Bernhard, but Bernhard never left the company to make way for Chuck, and never would. Chuck? No way. Bernhard had only made that promise to get at Faith. Ungrateful bitch!

Napoleon Brothers was not just any cesspit, it was Bernhard's cesspit and he was proud of it. Bernhard found the surveillance camera footage from the hospital wonderful viewing. If only Chuck had not thrown the towel over the camera. At least he still had the audio. Bernhard would love to have seen Faith's reaction when Chuck gave her the calf's testicles. Somewhat conveniently, Bernhard had just happened to have some in his office fridge. Donating them to Chuck had seemed the right thing to do.

"Knowing others is intelligence; knowing yourself is true wisdom. Mastering others is strength, mastering yourself is true power." ~ Lao-Tzu

Chapter 15

Four days later

The sun is setting on the majestic nearly purple mountain majesty of the outer Himalayas. A high dark storm front is outlined by the day's last rays. Storm clouds tower over the Kangra regional airport.

The small Indian airport is quiet and practically deserted. Faith and David disembark from the small, chartered aircraft. They have just flown through the storm, and it has left Faith sweaty, disheveled, and nauseous. Her Armani suit has an uncharacteristic stain on it.

The Indian pilot walks past Faith towards the back of the plane. Faith spits on the ground in front of him. The pilot glares angrily back at her and spits at Faith's feet before he savagely opens the baggage compartment.

He removes one of Faith's bags and throws it high up in the air to unload it. He does this with each of her bags and there are many. With a lighter bag, he throws it in the air twice. Fundamentally, Faith has a lot of baggage. The extra weight had almost killed them all. A strong gust of wind plucks at their clothes. The storm is closing in. There is a rumble of thunder.

Nearby, the few passengers from the final commercial flight of the day, a little 12-seat plane, disembark. The last passenger off is a bruised and sore Tenzin who stands at the top of the stairs looking out pensively before she painfully makes her way down to

63

the tarmac. Faith notices her immediately. There is something about her that grabs Faith's attention. The nun is greeted warmly, tenderly, by an older nun. They seem melancholy.

The arrival of the taxi distracts Faith. Two young Tibetan monks rush out and greet Faith. They give her a white khata scarf, hold their hands to their foreheads, and bow. They keep repeating the same phrase, which includes their entire English vocabulary. "Hello! Tashi Delek" "Hello! Tashi Delek!"

Faith responds stiffly, bowing her head just a smidge. She takes the scarf and, not knowing what to do with it, scrunches it up and stuffs it unceremoniously into her shoulder bag. David bows his head and solemnly places the scarf around his neck.

Faith's face is almost as threatening as the storm, and she can't stop rubbing the skin on her thumb. It was an itch she could never seem to scratch.

Faith looks at the taxi and shakes her head. There is not enough room in the taxi for Faith's luggage. It sounds and feels like it is about to start pouring. Faith searches for other options, any other option, but there are none. The young monks are oblivious; they happily carry her heavy bags to the vehicle. Each time the monks come back to the taxi they greet her, "Hello! Tashi Delek."

The boot cannot close; the lid has been tied down with a grimy piece of rope. The monks are trying to strap two large bags on the roof when Tenzin, carrying her small backpack, walks slowly past. The sight of Faith and the overloaded cab makes her smile. It is then that Faith notices that Tenzin has two different colored eyes, and she can't help staring at her.

The older nun talks to the two monks for a minute. She smiles at them and addresses Faith. "Dorje tells me that you are going to McLeod Ganj. We can take some of your luggage for you, save it getting soaked. He also tells me that you have made a generous donation to the Tibetan Children's Village, thank you for that, things have been a little difficult lately. We'll be back in just a minute."

It starts to rain and Faith scurries into the front seat, leaving David to assist with all the suitcases. David travels quite lightly, well, lightly compared to Faith.

Faith is relieved to exit the taxi and find a Five Star Hotel waiting for her. Chonor House is a unique boutique hotel owned by the Tibetan Government. It blends in with the hills overlooking the Kangra Valley. The building and decoration involved the work of three different groups of Tibetan painters. The murals, furniture, and décor vibrate with Tibetan authenticity. Faith is greeted by the Manager, a tall handsome Tibetan man with a dazzling smile.

"Welcome to Chonor House Ms. McCormack. Your suite is ready and a bath with soothing essential oils is being run for you." Faith smiles as he takes her hand to help her up the steps. The doorman, wearing a colorful Tibetan robe, opens the door for her.

"Thank you for your generous donation to the Tibetan Children's Village. The orphans and children will benefit greatly from your generosity." Faith squirms a little at the thanks but nods in acknowledgment. The donation had been more strategic than generous. She had arranged it along with some publicity to help open doors. She had not expected so much gratitude.

"The two monks who picked you up from the airport were orphans who grew up in the village. They asked if they could greet you. I trust they looked after you?" Faith nods her head. The two beaming monks bow and leave.

Faith twitches as she tries to get to sleep. She switches twitches for fidgeting but that doesn't help. She pretends to be asleep, but she doesn't fool anyone, not herself, not in this regard anyway. Sleep does not have to run very fast to elude her tonight. In utter exasperation, she gets out of bed and turns on the light.

The suite she is staying in could have been in Tibet. The precious polished rosewood, the elegant murals of the Tibetan countryside, and the Buddhist thangkas blend together in stylish harmony. But, instead of reveling in it, Faith feels as though the room is trying to smother her. She knows how to fix that.

Faith finds her smallest toiletry bag. In it are three bottles of sleeping tablets, two are empty and in the last one, there is only one-half tablet left. She shakes her head in disappointment. Faith goes to the minibar and opens a mini bottle of Jack Daniels.

The warning on the bottle of sleeping tablets is printed in a large bold red font, "Do not mix with alcohol." Faith is not color blind, but she is warning blind. She swallows the tablet, guzzles the Jack, and slips back under the warm covers. Moonlight shines through her window and Faith stares into it as she gets sleepier and sleepier… and drifts into a dream…

A full moon shines down on the smoldering ruins of a large, holy Tibetan monastery that is surrounded by the Chinese People's Liberation Army. A troop of soldiers drag a nun out of the carnage. A brace of ugly, squat tanks overlook the scene. The barrels of the tanks glow red. No stone was going to be left standing. Smoke and the smell of cordite hang heavy in the air. It overwhelms the subtle, but incredibly sad smell of an ancient culture being burnt to ash. Genocide stinks.

The nun's robes are ripped and bloodied. Her hands are tied behind her back. She is forced to stand next to two other injured nuns in front of an open pit.

Soldiers on the other side of the pit calmly finish their cigarettes and flick the butts on the ground before they raise their rifles. The nuns lift their heads, defiantly. The nun dragged from the ruins resembles Faith, albeit Faith with a butch haircut and blood running from under an eye that had looked too closely at the butt of a rifle. An owl flies down and screeches, as they often do in dreams. Faith repeats a mantra over and over, "I dedicate myself to freeing Tibet and to the Dalai Lama. I dedicate myself to freeing Tibet and to the Dalai Lama. I dedicate myself ..."

There is a loud CRACK, CRACK, CRACK...

Faith jolts awake, greedily gulping in deep breaths of air. She tentatively checks her chest for bullet holes and is relieved to find none. She is dripping with sweat even though it is a cold night. There is another loud CRACK from nearby, which makes Faith jump.

Trying to find the source of the sound, Faith draws back her curtains. She shies from the sudden bright light. The sun is high in the sky.

Nearby she can see one of the cleaners enthusiastically whacking a carpet to get the dust out of it. There is another loud CRACK. Faith is highly disturbed by the dream; it had seemed so real. Looking out on the conifer-clad hillside outside her room helps calm her. Time to get ready. Game time.

"Always forgive your enemies; nothing annoys them so much." ~ Oscar Wilde

Chapter 16

While waiting in the foyer of the Chonor Hotel, Faith looks at a large sparkling Swarovski cut crystal bowl sitting on top of a display cabinet. A face suddenly appears in every facet of the bowl. It is the face of a wizened, wrinkled, old Tibetan man with a long grey beard and mustache. A set of well-worn and ancient-looking prayer beads hang around his neck. He is dignified and exudes a calming presence. His left-hand rests on a polished walking stick.

He moves from the opposite side of the cabinet and bows to Faith. "Tashi Delek, Ms. McCormack. My name is Jampa, and I will be your guide while you are here in McLeod Ganj."

Jampa's English sounds British, but his gap-toothed smile is pure Tibetan. Faith puts out her hand to shake hands which Jampa does. "Miss Faith, we have two hours until we can see His Eminence Chodrak Trungpa at Tushita Monastery. Would you like to go there now and meditate?"

Faith smiles in her special way. A way that is both patronizing and condescending. "Jumper, I don't meditate, I'm too busy to waste time on that. I want you to tell me everything you know about how reincarnations are found."

Jampa stays silent but his raised eyebrows speak volumes. David just looks abashed. David had been busy. The Manager had highly recommended Jampa and David had moved swiftly to secure his services. He follows Faith and Jampa into the hotel restaurant.

Faith is drinking her third latte as she drums her fingers on the table. She stops only to make a note in her Palm Pilot. Her copy of '*The Tibetan Book of Living and Dying*' is off to one side of the table. Jampa sips his tea while David is reading The Times of India.

Faith puts down her had held computer and looks at Jampa. "Let me see if I've got this right. There are two basic types of recognized reincarnations; A) Those that are actively searched for like the ...Dalai Lama and the Panchen Lama, and B) Those that are discovered later and found to be reincarnations of important past persons. Tooolku's?"

Jampa grimaces and opens his mouth to interject but Faith continues, carried away with her own cleverness. She was really getting the hang of Buddhism. "So... all I have to do is get my name on the 'A' list! Just like Hollywood. How much do you think that will cost, Jumper?" Jampa shakes his head and chuckles.

"I think, Miss Faith, that you have much to learn about Tibetan Buddhism. We should be going now." Jampa rises and makes his way to the door.

The drive to Tushita Monastery is short but the strands of *lung dar* prayer flags that they pass on the way are long, very long: so many prayers. The flags are all arranged in a specific order; blue represents the sky, white for air, red for fire, green symbolizes water, and yellow represents earth and all five colors together signify balance.

They have to stop frequently for people walking on the narrow streets of McLeod Ganj. Once out of town, the road gets much steeper.

Faith has never seen non-human monkeys before, and she is fascinated by them. They stop so she can take a photo of a handwritten sign with two arrows on it. One arrow points to a path going back down the hill, it says, 'Short way to McLeod Ganj' and above it, the other arrow, pointing in the other direction says, 'Short way to enlightenment.' The rest of the drive goes swiftly.

After parking the car, they walk towards the monastery which is nestled in the hills above McLeod Ganj. It is a relatively small monastery that can accommodate a hundred people. In Tibet, before the Chinese invasion, there were monasteries the size of small cities that could accommodate as many as 10,000 monks. Sadly, only six out of 6,000 ancient Tibetan monasteries survived the Cultural Revolution.

As they approach the main entrance, a monk, Monk Tsultrim steps forward and greets Jampa and shakes his hands warmly. They touch foreheads. He then bows to Faith and David and shakes their hands too. The monk takes them into a room and motions for them to sit on cushions while they wait.

"His Eminence is with someone. You will be called when he is ready to see you."

Jampa takes two carefully folded, pure white scarfs from his bag. He gives one to Faith and one to David. Despite the cane, Jampa sits gracefully into the lotus position and wraps his prayer beads around his wrist. He gestures to Faith to sit next to him. She remains standing instead. Faith looks at her watch and puts the khata around her neck. It is five minutes to 11 AM.

"No point sitting down, we'll be going in… in five minutes."

Jampa reminds Faith, "Tsultrim will get us when His Eminence is ready to receive us. He is a busy man." After a long pause, he adds, "You may find it easier to take your watch off." Faith begins to pace.

"The white silk material I have given you is called a khata." Jampa takes one from his pocket and holds it up. "If you look closely, you can see that there are auspicious symbols woven into the fabric. Giving of the khata is a simple ritual that is a gesture of respect and good intentions."

Jampa takes his khata and folds it in half lengthwise. "It is folded thus, and when you offer it to his Eminence you place it over your hands like this, with the folded section facing you which represents your open heart, with no negative thoughts or…" and Jampa adds special emphasis on the next word, "…motives."

"The traditional way to offer the khata is from near your forehead with a humble bow, with your head bent, and your palms joined in respect." Jampa demonstrates this for them. "Often you will receive your khata back."

Simple rituals can sound complex when they are new and when the person wants to honor the rite and is a perfectionist it can lead to anxiety. Jampa can see that David is looking concerned; if Faith has heard him, he cannot tell. Faith is busy making faces at a three-eyed demon on one of the thangkas on the wall. Jampa reassures David, "In all my experience with ritual David, your intention is much more important than getting the fine details right."

Jampa closes his eyes and begins to pray with his prayer beads. The beads move swiftly through his fingers. The fingers that move the prayer beads are mangled, and missing fingernails. Jampa must have done a lot of hard, physical labor in his time.

Faith alternates between pacing and checking her watch. She inspects the various wall hangings. Finally, she sits down and looks at her watch. She picks up her book and checks her watch again. She taps it even though she knows it is working. Faith is getting increasingly agitated.

At 11:20 she gets up and walks over to Jampa. As Faith reaches out to tap Jampa on the shoulder, Jampa says, "Take your watch off. It will help you to at least try to calm your mind."

Behind Jampa's back Faith makes a face at Jampa, and silently mouths his words in a very childish form of defiance.

"Miss Faith, it will benefit you in your audience."

A man in a worn, plain chuba arrives with Monk Tsultrim. He smiles and nods to each of them in a friendly and open way. Calmly he sits down, takes out his prayer beads and starts to pray.

Faith gets her Palm Pilot out and starts to jab aggressively at the screen. She crosses out 'Offer Tibetans US$25 million to find reincarnation.' After a satisfying pause, she retypes it with forceful pokes, but the 25 is reduced to 20. David continues sitting calmly, reading legal documents from his briefcase.

At 11:45, Faith crosses out the 20 and replaces it with 18. After another bout of pacing, she clenches her fists and storms to the inner chamber door.

Faith flings open the massive, creaky, intricately carved wooden door. His Eminence sits on a cushion under a large golden statue of Buddha. On the altar above him is a photo of the Dalai Lama and pictures of other esteemed teachers. The smell of incense hovers in the air and candles burn gently in their holders.

An old Tibetan woman sits in front of His Eminence as he chants and reads from a sutra that is on a low table before him. Monk Tsultrim sits to the left of His Eminence. Obviously, there is more than one way into the room. They all look up in surprise at the sudden intrusion.

Faith is framed in the doorway by the bright sunlight that streams from behind her. Faith holds up her wrist and points to her watch. Jampa grabs her wrist and pulls it to her side. He bows his head.

In Tibetan, Jampa says, "Your Eminence, please pardon this rude interruption." His Eminence, who is an old man, starts to laugh. It is a warm, genuine laugh. He replies in Tibetan to Jampa, "So Jampa, you bring an impatient western leopard to see me?"

"No, Your Eminence, a leopard would starve if it did not learn patience. You will not be disturbed again."

Outside, when Faith finally stops pacing, she fumes instead. Jampa is now sitting with his back to the door that Faith had charged through. His eyes are closed but the prayer beads continue to click rapidly through his fingers. The regular, practiced clicking of prayer beads by Jampa and the old Tibetan man, calms David in a way that Faith would never understand. David has to bite his lip to stop himself from laughing at her antics.

Monk Tsultrim enters the antechamber with a tray of steaming butter tea and tsampa, which is ground-roasted barley. He nods to Jampa and whispers in the old man's ear. Jampa holds the door open for them. The old man carries his khata on his hands as he enters the room. Jampa quickly closes the door behind them and resumes his vigil.

The muffled sound of laughter comes from within the room. The time is 12:30 PM according to Faith's Palm Pilot. Her offer is now down to US$12 million, followed by a question mark, followed by another question mark.

Propped up against a wall, Faith has just started to doze when the Palm Pilot low battery warning starts to whine. It is 1:25 PM. The door opens shortly afterward, and the old man and woman leave together. They are both wearing khatas around their necks. Both bow and offer blessings back toward His Eminence as they leave the room. The old woman is so happy that tear trails are visible on her face.

Monk Tsultrim beckons for them to enter the room. His Eminence sits on a cushion and smiles at them. Faith quickens her pace and walks in front of Jampa. She places the khata on her hands as she was shown and makes a very curt, perfunctory bow. David presents his khata and then Jampa comes forward. His Eminence holds Jampa's hands before taking the khata which he returns to him.

The visitors sit on cushions in a semi-circle facing His Eminence. Chodrak Trungpa rearranges his robes and then looks Faith steadily in the eye. Faith is furious but she cannot hold eye contact which makes her even more upset. She averts her gaze and looks at where her watch would normally be. She clears her throat and the dam bursts. "I have been waiting for nearly three hours!"

Jampa translates this into Tibetan though it hardly requires it. His Eminence takes this outburst calmly. There is a definite twinkle in his eyes. He replies in Tibetan which Jampa translates into English. "Yes, and you do it very poorly. Obviously, you need more practice." Monk Tsultrim is trying hard to keep a straight face.

"Do you know who I am?" Jampa translates this and His Eminence looks deeply into, Faith holding her gaze, which makes her squirm. The prayer beads in his hands continue moving bead by bead. It is some time before he answers.

"I see before me a very scared woman ... and I see suffering and pain, much pain." Jampa translates this verbatim. Faith looks surprised, she fidgets. That was not the answer she was looking for.

"Look... um, Your Eminence. I am Faith McCormack." Jampa translates this into Tibetan. There is no reaction. "I am one of the richest people on this planet."

Jampa dutifully translates. His Eminence clears his throat a couple of times, blinks and wraps, and then rewraps his prayer beads around his hand.

"And has your wealth brought you great happiness and peace?" The question causes Faith to stop and think. She is about to answer when she remembers her purpose.

"Your Eminence, I didn't come here for therapy. I came here because I have a problem..." Faith pauses dramatically but the drama is for personal consumption. "I am dying. I have no time to waste."

Jampa translates. His Eminence looks at her and again Faith cannot look back into the pools of peace that are his eyes. From somewhere nearby bells start to ring. At the sound, His Eminence stands up and smiles. He adjusts his robes.

"No one has any time to waste. No one. You see, we are all dying, every moment is precious. But dying is not a problem, it is easy to do, everyone dies." His Eminence laughs. Jampa does not have to translate the farewell. "Tashi Delek."

Chodrak Trungpa turns and starts to leave the room. Jampa and David bow, as does Monk Tsultrim. Faith is confounded. When she gets to her feet, instead of bowing, she rushes after His Eminence and actually scoots in front of him to stop him from leaving.

"Wait, Your Eminence, please, just wait a minute." Monk Tsultrim is shocked by her behavior. Jampa goes to Faith's side and tries to remove her from His Eminence's path. His Eminence indicates that it is OK.

"I have only four to five months left to live." Jampa translates. His Eminence is about to say something, but Faith interrupts him. "I have a contract here. I will pay the Tibetan Government 25 million US dollars if you will find my reincarnation."

After Jampa finishes, His Eminence stops and inspects Faith. He can see that she is serious. He softens his look and smiles. With great compassion, he responds.

"Ms. McCormack, death is a great opportunity to release attachment to all worldly possessions. If all your money has not brought you happiness in this lifetime, why do you suppose it will be different in your next lifetime?" Jampa translates as His Eminence is speaking. There is a pause and His Eminence continues, "Use the time you have left to prepare yourself for..."

Faith does not let him finish, "OK, OK, I was lowballing you, 28 million dollars. 25% payable on the signing of the contract and then..." As Jampa translates, Faith can see that His Eminence is not the slightest bit interested which is why she trails off. Jampa grabs her arm firmly.

"Achala, I give you a blessing for your great journey." His Eminence lays his hand on her head, chants, and then walks off. Faith yells after him, "My final offer is 34 million dollars - that's it, no more..." Jampa does not bother to translate this nor the expletive that she finishes with. "Shit!"

Faith stamps her feet in great frustration. David is extremely embarrassed. Faith turns and glares at him. "What? What?"

Chuck Jones is still on the Napoleon Brothers' board and in the same senior job but with extra responsibility and a substantial pay increase. All the traders that had worked for Faith now report to Chuck. That could have been a source of satisfaction but Chucky, primed from his performance at the hospital, had bragged long and loud to everyone he could corner about his impending promotion to CEO. The ultimate promotion for him but one that was nothing more than a Bernhard Napoleon mind game.

Few believed Chuck or even gave it a second thought. Bernhard would leave Napoleon Brothers in a rainforest-felled cedar box, not before but Chuck's recent display of his delusions of grandeur made him, rightly, feel like a fool. It dented his inflated pride which had already been soiled by that witch woman. Chuck was determined to restore his reputation. What he needed was a big win in the market, a big one, bigger even than McCormack's gold play.

"Does the walker choose the path, or the path the walker?" ~ Garth Nix

Chapter 17

Faith and David are walking up a hill; they are following a smiling Jampa towards Ganden Monastery. It is a larger monastery than Tushita. Their heads are high. Faith is smiling and she holds a copy of the contract in her hand as if it was her Holy Grail. It is cold but sunny.

Sometime later Faith stomps back down the hill whilst David runs after. David is carrying the contract. Jampa, still smiling, is last; he shakes his head. The day has turned cloudy.

Faith is nothing if not insensitive and persistent. Over the following two weeks, at different monasteries in northern India, the scenes at Tushita and Ganden Monasteries are repeated with a few more and a few less embarrassing variations.

Faith is stumped, she just can't work it out. Finding reincarnations was part of the Tibetan religion so why not find one for a very large cheque? If this was Chicago, she would be swamped with offers. In fact, she would probably be in hiding.

The Tibetans didn't want anything from her. She wasn't sure if money had suddenly become mute, but it certainly wasn't doing the talking that she was used to. BUT it only took one person to break ranks for Faith to get what she wanted. Strangely enough, the more they said 'no,' the more determined Faith was that she wanted the Tibetans to find her next self. Faith had always had a strong contrary streak.

The long drives and the stress of not getting what she wanted were not helping her medical condition. She was shaking more and more frequently and ... umm, yes, staying focused was becoming more challenging.

Jampa had taken Faith to a Tibetan Doctor who had given her some tablets which seemed to be helping? Maybe? Probably not. She didn't have high hopes for any medical help, but she had gone along with it because... because Jampa had suggested it. She had found that when she was with Jampa, she felt calmer, better.

David did not accompany them to all the monasteries. He was focused on consolidating Faith's wealth, liquidating certain assets, and reallocating others, rolling everything into a very, very large trust fund.

India would not have been his first choice of country for doing this. It wouldn't have been his last choice either. The 9-and-a-half-hour time difference was unhelpful and the phone lines and internet connections in regional areas were temperamental to say the best about them. Fortunately, he had a fantastic team working for him back in the States.

What was more challenging than connectivity to deal with were the frequent Faith-clones. Faith-clones had the intensity of cyclones, but these were high-intensity, emotional storms where Faith would vacillate from leaving everything to David to take care of, to wanting to control the minutiae of every detail herself. A complete emotional cycle could take two days or two hours. Her highs were high, and her lows were very low. None of this was typical of the Faith he knew. Though she still tried to hide it, her hands were constantly shaking.

Jampa and Faith are waiting in another waiting room in yet another monastery. This one was set deep in the forest and felt especially peaceful. To be honest, they all felt peaceful even after Faith had visited. Chanting can be heard in the distance as well as the sound of Tibetan cymbals. Jampa is sitting serenely, prayer beads moving through his fingers. He is trying to talk to Faith. "But..."

"Look Jampa, no buts. I want to see all the senior lamas until one of them says 'yes.' You are doing a great job getting me appointments. It's not your fault that they say 'no' and are not very punctual."

"But, Miss Faith, there is something I need to tell you..."

"Uh, uh ... no more buts Jampa, trust me, I can sell ice cream to Inuits. You just keep opening the doors for me."

As she finishes saying this, the doors to the reception room open and a monk escorts them to some cushions that are situated on the floor in front of a simple platform. Two monks stand respectfully beside a five-year-old boy who is sitting on a raised cushion on the platform.

Behind the boy, the entire wall is one giant glass cabinet divided into 10 sections. Inside the bottom five partitions are bronze statues of Buddha each with an orange robe over the left shoulder. Each statue is as large as the boy. Of the top sections, the three middle ones also have statues of Buddha in them.

Faith walks briskly ahead of Jampa, totally focused on her sales pitch. When Faith gets to the cushions on the floor she looks up at the throne and is about to bow and present the khata when she notices that the figure sitting there is a child.

Faith looks around and then steps forward. "You cheeky boy. Shoo, go on." Faith speaks very slowly for the boy's benefit. "We are here for a very important business meeting ... business." Clearly, the boy does not speak corporate and Jampa has not bothered to interpret what she has said. "Now you better run off before you get into big trouble ..."

The boy Rinpoche laughs and claps his hands in delight. Jampa moves past Faith. He bows and presents his khata to the young Lama. The boy places the khata over Jampa's neck. Jampa bows again and stares at Faith. David follows Jampa. Faith is stunned.

The boy Rinpoche is thoroughly enjoying himself. He has a smile that is infectious unless, like Faith, your rapidly burning sense of embarrassment gives you immunity. He proclaims loudly, "I like her, she is funny."

"If all economists were laid end to end, they would not reach a conclusion." ~ *George Bernard Shaw*

Chapter 18

In the hotel restaurant David has just finished his meal, and his plate is empty. Faith has hardly touched any of her food. She is tired and not well. She is even having difficulty typing a simple note into her Palm Pilot.

"Explain to me again, David, why we didn't go straight to the Dalai Lama?"

"Faith, he is in retreat, and no one will disturb him."

Faith starts to rub her arm where her blouse touches her skin while she is trying to concentrate on her Palm Pilot. "For a deal like this, you'd think they would shake him out of retreat and into action." She presses a key and appears pleased with herself. She looks cunningly at David.

"This is good news... yes. Cheryl – you remember Cheryl? My old assistant?" David was pretty sure that this was a rhetorical question, but he shakes his head in the negative which makes no difference. Faith blithely continues... "She has just confirmed my suspicions. The rupee is vulnerable, at least in the very short term anyway. David, patch me through to the Prime Minister of India... first thing tomorrow morning."

David looks sharply at Faith, his eyes widening in horror. "What? No, no way!"

Faith fires one word at her lawyer, "PICASSO." David flinches. He was beginning to wonder if the painting was worth it, maybe it was cursed? He had never heard of any of Picasso's works being cursed but then... note to self: Check if any Picasso's had a curse on them.

"Oh David, don't be a baby, just do it! Threaten, bribe, lie, whatever. My track record in smashing currencies should be more than enough to get you through. Do not take 'no' for an answer. Tell them that I am trying to stop Napoleon Brothers from leading a massive run on the rupee. Let's see if we can put a little 'host nation' pressure on our dear Tibetan refugee friends." David has gone green. It is not the food nor is it envy.

Cheryl was surprised to get the phone call from Faith asking her to make a series of trades on Faith's personal accounts. Short-term trades. Everything had happened so fast that whilst all of Faith's outstanding trades had been closed out, her trading accounts had not been canceled, and Cheryl was still an authorized agent for Faith.

Faith had sounded different. She had been, well... polite and had even asked how Cheryl was. That was new. Cheryl was happy to oblige. She had made so much money from backing Faith's *coup de grace* gold deal with her own money that she didn't have to work ever again. She had no love for Faith, but Faith had treated her fairly. She had also encouraged Cheryl to start trading herself. Encouraged? Well, she'd told her to.

Cheryl had been in the office when Chuck had returned from ambushing Faith in the hospital. He was tripping on power. He reeked of bourbon and testosterone gone wrong. Cheryl may have imagined it, but when he gloated about how he had pulled on the drip in Faith's arm, his eyes had seemed to glow red like a TV demon's, or maybe it was just all the alcohol that made his eyes bloodshot. Either way, it still made Cheryl shudder.

From her sources within the company, she knew that Chuck's behavior was not an isolated act of extreme malice. She knew enough about Chuck to make her want to... vomit. She hated big, fat, red-necked, chauvinistic bullies with a passion, so she had stayed on to see if an opportunity might arise to give Chuck some well-deserved payback. The nice thing was that if things didn't work out, she could bail at any time.

Faith is in her suite on the phone. She is wearing her self-satisfied, 'I got what I wanted' look. David watches and winces. "Yes, thank you, Mr. Prime Minister. I am enjoying my time here in your country but some of your information is incorrect. I have certainly left the Napoleon Brothers sewer, but I have not retired, how could I? I distributed certain... rumors to divert attention away from me so I could come here to investigate the Indian rupee firsthand. Yes... it is fascinating, and I wanted to get out of Chicago... hmm well, unfortunately, I have some bad news for your economy, the rupee is looking defenseless... but if you can help me, perhaps I can help you... Why would I help? Well, as they say, any enemy of Napoleon Brothers is my friend..."

Though it had started pleasantly, the conversation was not going the way that Faith had anticipated, and she is quickly exasperated. "Oh, yes, I see... uh-huh, I realize that the Tibetans consider it a..." she spits the next words out, "a spiritual matter and... so even though they are refugees in your country helping my 'friend' is totally out of your control?" There is a pause, a short pause because the question has already been answered.

"Oh, the rupee? Well ... that is outside my control ... sorry, Mr. Prime Minister, my battery is about to go, thank you for your time," and with that Faith throws the phone across the room, which pulls the cord from the wall socket and makes a loud and satisfying bang. The wall that was on the receiving end of the phone will need repairing.

"Maybe we can find someone else to find your next incarnation?" suggests David.

Faith is trembling with rage, "I don't trust anybody else. I trust you and these... these Tibetans. I don't know why... Well, I know why I trust you." Suddenly Faith's rage turns to tears.

David finds he is more comfortable with her rage, than her vulnerability but he goes to Faith and holds her, just holds her while the fury drips out, tear by tear. This was going to make what he had to do even harder.

Later that night, in the restaurant, as the waiter leaves them having topped up their beautiful teacups with green tea, David noisily clears his throat. Faith knows David well enough to know that the throat clearing is a plucking up courage action rather than a phlegm-related response.

He looks at Faith and in a forced casual, conversational tone says, "Maybe it's time to see a specialist again." This was not what Faith was expecting, and she looks up.

"What are you trying to say, David?" David sighs and whilst he has a sudden desire to clear his throat again, he resists. "Look... this ..." There is another sigh, and a sudden buildup of phlegm makes him cough.

"You have a brain-wasting disease Faith and this... this obsession is, well, it is madness." Faith waits for him to clear his throat again which he does. This was serious. "You will reach a point in this disease where you will be legally considered to be *non compos mentis*. Not of sound mind." David pauses again and looks away, "Maybe we're already there."

"Me? *Non compos mentis*? Just because I made you ring the Prime Minister of India to help me out?" David just stares at Faith which makes her blush. OK, she concedes to herself that maybe that was a bit mad.

"Look, I'm fine, really.   Really.   A bit frustrated, admittedly." Faith's hand shakes noticeably. She grips it with her other hand to still it.

Defensively, Faith continues, "Listen, you suggested this option."

"No, Faith. No, I didn't. Don't try that on me. You did. I mean ... how many 'nos' does it take for you to get it?"

Faith skewers David with a look. "You've obviously never had to really fight for anything, David. If I had taken 'no' as an answer I would never be where I am now."

David has to build up courage before he softly says, "And just where are you, Faith? Where are you? You're wasting what little time you have left ..."

"Don't you dare patronize me."

David studies the tea leaves at the bottom of his cup. They looked like a random scattering of tiny mouse pellets to him. Maybe he could read tea leaves? Because he was certainly feeling like shit. Finally, he looks up.

"Faith, I'm leaving, tomorrow."

Faith is stunned.   She relied on David's support and companionship more than she admitted. The look of a hurt abandoned little girl steals across her face.

"You can't leave me."

"Faith, I can't help you here anymore. To finalize the trust arrangements, I need to be back in the States and me, well, I have a family to get back to in Chicago. My youngest daughter just broke her leg…"

Faith feels abandoned. David carefully puts his serviette on the table. In a forced jovial tone, he reassures Faith, "You'll be fine. 'Jumper' is with you, and I'll be in daily contact or as daily contact as the phone system here will allow… Good night Faith."

David gets up. He hesitates, then gives Faith a kiss on the head before he walks out of the restaurant. Faith remains rigidly upright but once David is out of sight, she crumples. Even in her pain she understood, but going? He was going? Leaving with David was also the constant and welcome financial distraction of consolidating her trust fund.

Bernhard enjoyed having Chuck around, he was like a large, amusing, slightly unhinged lap dog but with Faith gone, he was more risk than reward. Chuck would need to be put down, but there was no hurry because perversely, since Faith had 'left,' Chuck had started making more money for the company than he had ever made before, and the internal controls would prevent him from doing anything crazy.

Unfortunately for Bernhard, the call from the Indian Finance Minister was put through to Chuck as he was the only board member in the building at the time. It was a strange call. Chuck confirmed for the Minister that Faith no longer worked for Napoleon Brothers, and he took some delight in telling him that she had been sacked, which was a lie, and that she was dying from new variant Creutzfeldt-Jakob Disease, which was not.

The Minister told him that Faith had claimed that she had not retired but was doing currency research in India. He would not say more, just that he was ringing just to verify a few facts. It was a short and strange call.

Interesting, thought Chuck, very interesting. He was excited. It made him rub his chubby, sweaty hands together. There was more to this. He could smell an opportunity, but he needed to find out everything that Faith had said to the Indian Prime Minister. She had evidently ruffled a few feathers, typical. Shouldn't she be dead by now? A few bribes in the right hands would get him the information he required. He just needed someone to do the research work and wire transfers for him.

When Chuck jerks open the door to his office, he realizes that it must be later than he had thought. There are only two people still at their desks, an unattractive woman he had never noticed before and his office manager, Stephen. The duckling that had obstinately stayed ugly was wearing headphones.

Discretion as a word or concept had discreetly avoided appearing in Chuck's limited vocabulary. Even so, Chuck decides to use his inside voice to brief Stephen on the 'little job' he had for him.

As he stalks back into his lair, Chuck thinks that maybe he should have called Stephen into his office to talk to him. He thinks this because the sight of the woman tapping her foot to music irritated him. If a duckling couldn't turn into a beautiful swan, then they could swim in someone else's pond.

Cheryl heard everything because whilst her headphones were on her head, the music was off and Chuck's inside-the-office voice was locker room loud; he had never learned to whisper.

At the right time, Cheryl would offer to do all the dirty work for Stephen who was easily as lazy and almost as incompetent as his boss. She knew that all trades through Chuck's Napoleon-controlled accounts were carefully monitored and reported daily to the board. She also knew that Faith's more extensive Napoleon Brothers brokerage accounts had been largely forgotten since Faith's spectacular departure. Faith's accounts had never had a high level of oversight. They could be useful and there was no way to access them except from inside the Napoleon Brothers secure network. Cheryl had no doubt that Chuck would find that interesting when Stephen told him.

*"Something opens our wings. Something makes
boredom and hurt disappear. Someone fills the
cup in front of us: We taste only sacredness." ~
Rumi*

Chapter 19

Faith and Jampa are sitting in front of a door, waiting. This was the newest monastery they had visited, it even smelled new. Jampa as usual sits straight-backed in the lotus position. His prayer beads click steadily through his fingers. His eyes are closed; his regular breathing is peaceful. Faith sits with her shoulders slumped, her forehead resting on her drawn-up knees. She is very unhappy, and vulnerable. Self-doubt and regret take turns attacking her psyche.

"Jampa? Jampa, are there any more after this one?" Jampa opens his eyes and solemnly holds up one finger.

"I may have to ..." Faith sighs heavily. "I don't know. I don't know anything anymore. My gut feeling was so strong about this and when I have followed it in the past it has never let me down. I've made a cock-up of everything, haven't I?"

Jampa pats the cushion next to him. With some physical difficulty, Faith moves across and sits next to Jampa. Jampa leans across and places his prayer beads in her hands. Faith holds them, feels their weight, and she looks at them closely. They were so smooth, they felt... exquisite, like love on a string. She looks up at Jampa.

"Where's the 'On' switch?" Jampa points to his head and then his heart. He places her fingers on the bead nearest the red tuft of thread where the knot is.

"Start with this one. One prayer, one bead, 108 beads. Batteries not required and each prayer is totally recyclable." They both smile. Faith looks up at him questioning.

"Ahh, the prayer I use is 'Om Mani Padme Hum,' it is the Tibetan prayer of compassion, wishing for the end of suffering for all sentient beings." Faith gives a weak smile.

"Hmmm ... maybe I should start with one that is a little more selfish?" This time it is Jampa who smiles. Faith's fingers start to slowly move the prayer beads.

Sometime later Jampa and Faith walk out through the same door that they had been waiting in front of. Faith is sickly pale, and her movements take a lot of effort. They are jerky and awkward. She looks at Jampa who is supporting her and with a forced grin she says, "Apparently we are all dying." Jampa smiles at Faith. "Thank you Jampa. Thank you for staying with me."

Faith walks behind Jampa. They are approaching the last monastery on Faith's list. The 'lucky' last is the largest in India. Up close it is even more impressive than it is from a distance. Yeshe Trichen Rinpoche had only recently returned from a series of lectures in Europe. This was more like it.

As they enter Faith looks around and nods her head approvingly at the quality of the furnishings in the room. Monk Tsering greets them warmly.

"Ahhhh cha. You are here to see Rinpoche?" Jampa bows his head.

"Please follow me."

As they walk, Faith says to Jampa, "Finally! This is more like it. They should sack all those other guys, except maybe the kid, he's obviously fairly new." Jampa shakes his head. Thanks to Faith his neck muscles were the strongest they had ever been.

Once they leave the main building, they begin to climb up a steep, narrow path through the conifers. Monkeys chatter in the branches. They stop regularly for Faith to watch the primates and to catch her breath. Fortunately, it does not take long to arrive at a ridge, where the ground levels out. Up ahead they see a cave that commands a spectacular view over the valley. As good as it was, Faith did not consider the outlook worth the effort required to get to it. A strong cool breeze rustles through the trees.

As they near the cave, they see Yeshe Trichen Rinpoche sitting on a simple cushion on the floor. A nun, Tenzin, is talking with him, kneeling and sitting comfortably back on her heels. Faith and Jampa are too far away to hear the conversation.

"But Rinpoche, if you and the other lamas together cannot unravel the prophecy what can I do? I was merely the messenger." Tenzin's head drops and her shoulders slump as she says this.

"Ani-La, what you can do is to believe in yourself. Every day your compassion is a gift to this world." Rinpoche pauses before continuing.

"This prophecy picked you to deliver it and you have done this, against overwhelming odds and at great personal cost. I believe, as do many others, that your role as messenger is a beginning rather than an end to your involvement."

Tenzin sits up straighter. She didn't believe that she was still connected, however, she was not going to argue with her teacher.

Faith and Jampa are standing at a respectful distance but the wind stops blowing and, in the stillness, they can now hear everything that is being said.

"Thank you, Rinpoche. Of course, I will continue to meditate on the prophecy whilst I am in retreat."

"Any insights you have, no matter how seemingly small or trivial, may be of inestimable value and I would like to hear of them as soon as possible." Tenzin nods her head in affirmation.

Rinpoche and Tenzin become aware of their guests. Rinpoche nods his head to Tenzin. She prostrates to Rinpoche and then gets up to leave. Rinpoche beams at the departing nun.

Though deep in thought, Tenzin smiles at the newcomers as she turns to go. Faith is transfixed. It was the nun from the airport, the one with the different colored eyes. Faith takes a few steps and is about to follow the nun when Jampa clears his throat and brings her back to the present. Faith is finding it harder and harder to concentrate.

They present their khatas to Rinpoche and take their seats on the cushions that are on the ground. After a pause, Faith clears her throat. "Rinpoche, thank you for meeting… um... seeing me." Faith has caught David's throat-clearing habit. "I have come to offer the Tibetan Government in Exile US$40 million dollars."

Jampa translates this into Tibetan. Rinpoche takes his glasses off and cleans them, slowly, deliberately. He looks intently at Faith before he speaks, "That is very, generous of you. Thank you. Many orphans' and refugees' lives will be saved as a result of your generosity."

Jampa translates this. Rinpoche bows to Faith, his prayer beads wrapped around his hands, and then he sits back up. There is a long silence. Faith starts to squirm and fidget. She can't maintain eye contact. She clears her throat a couple more times.

"Well... umm, yes... you're absolutely right. That kind of money will make a big difference... but, there is just one little condition..." Faith, having stumbled this far, pauses for breath and then rushes the sting, "You have to agree to find my reincarnation for me."

There is a long pause before Rinpoche replies "Hmmm... I see ... hmmm." He takes off his glasses, notices a small smudge, and cleans them again. Then he starts to laugh, it is a gorgeous laugh. He starts to laugh so hard that he is nearly crying.

He says to Jampa in Tibetan, "Jampa you scoundrel, what a wonderful joke. You almost tricked me. I thank you and this woman so much..."

Jampa, replies quickly in Tibetan, "Rinpoche, Rinpoche ... this is no joke, she is deadly serious, excuse the pun."

Faith is totally confused, she hisses to Jampa, "What did he say and why is he laughing so hard?" Jampa is smiling now, and Rinpoche's mirth is contagious. "Hmmm, well... umm. Rinpoche thought that this was a..." Jampa searches for the right word and misses, "A particular joke."

"Practical joke?"

"Hmmm... yes. I have been known to play some jokes on people." Rinpoche has difficulty composing himself. Somehow his glasses have got dirty again and taking them off makes it easier to wipe the moisture from his eyes. He sits up and assumes a straight face, a straight-ish face.

Rinpoche's face has many wrinkles, and the wrinkles are distributed in such a way that it always looks like he is about to laugh, which he does, frequently. He is not embarrassed by what has happened.

"Why would you want us to find your next incarnation?"

"Well... I'm dying and ..."

Rinpoche replies now in good English. "We are all dying."

Faith is taken aback but grateful to be speaking English. "Yes, yes, indeed, we are all dying. I know that. All dying. I just think it... would be a good thing... to do for me... karmically speaking." Faith looks down at the ground. Yeshe Trichen continues to stare calmly at her whilst praying with his prayer beads. He does not respond.

"So... Rinpoche how did they find your reincarnation?"

"Give me your hand."

Rinpoche takes Faith's hand and looks at it. He inspects it whilst periodically drilling her with his eyes. He takes her pulse. Faith finds this disconcerting.

"Achala, worrying and scheming about your next life, before you have even completed this one, is not a good practice." Faith pulls her hand back.

"Rinpoche, the offer I have made is very, very generous. The money, as you said, will save many lives, save a lot of suffering."

"Achala, to know that you are dying is a priceless gift. Amazingly, death comes as a surprise for most people, despite the fact that everyone knows soon after birth that one day they will die. Despite this knowledge, they do not prepare for death. As you approach death's door you will find that you cannot take anything with you, not even an American Express card. Attachment to worldly possessions at the time of death brings great challenges in the Bardo and can result in a less than favorable rebirth."

"Right ... yup, yeah. Well, I'm prepared to take that risk. Look, you're a busy man, I'm dying… and so is everyone else so let's cut to the chase, do we have a deal?" There is no reaction from Rinpoche.

"I may be able to increase it a little if that helps." Finally, Rinpoche smiles at her. "Achala, not everyone gets a precious human rebirth. What if you incarnate as a goat or a frog or a hungry ghost? Hmmm... What then?"

Faith drops the contract that she has been holding in surprise. She shakes her head, her brow furrows, and her frown is fierce. Say what?

"But... But that's not possible? You know, once human, always human."

"And where is your contract that says that? Hmmm? Some people may wait hundreds of years before being granted another precious human rebirth..." Rinpoche gives his words a moment to sink in and they do.

"There are highly evolved beings that have transcended the wheel of Samsara." Rinpoche can see that Faith is not following him. "They no longer have to experience the cycle of death and rebirth. These beings choose human rebirth to benefit all sentient beings. It is the reincarnation of these beings that we search for. No amount of money can buy such a holy position."

Faith stares at Rinpoche; she has a lot to think about. Finally, Faith looks away and she gets up, clumsily, ready to leave.

This was not going to happen here. Faith turns back to Rinpoche. "There are always exceptions to every rule."

"Achala ... If you pursued your spiritual nature with the vigor and dedication that you pursue money ... it is I ... who would be seated at your feet."

"When one does not understand death, life can be very confusing." ~ Ajahn Chah

Chapter 20

The path down from the cave seems much longer than it had on the way up. Near the bottom, Jampa gently leads a dejected Faith off the beaten track onto a hidden trail that takes them to a smooth rock outcrop on the edge of a cliff. The trees and valley below spread out in green glory, but Faith cannot see the forest for her pain. Faith looks at Jampa with raised eyebrows.

"Why are we here? Are you suggesting that I jump? Not a bad idea given my lack of success." Faith tries to use humor to mask how weak and afraid she is, but Jampa has always seen Faith for who she is. One of the many things she loved about Jampa was that she did not have to pretend with him, though it did not stop her trying. He accepted her, no matter her mood.

Jampa sits close to the edge. Faith hesitates, then carefully, cautiously she sits down and scootches along to his side. Jampa points to the now-tattered contract that Faith is still somehow clutching to her bosom. He opens the box that he has been carrying with him all day. Inside is a beautiful Tibetan singing bowl, a pen, a wooden block, an ink pad, and matches.

He gives the printing block to Faith and takes the contract from her. He turns the document upside down and, holding her hands, they press the block into the ink pad before firmly pushing it onto the last page. Jampa removes his hand, and Faith lifts up the block to see what she has printed. The image is an outline of a strong, bridled, beautifully proportioned horse but instead of having a rider, the horse's saddle has what looks like a flame coming out of it? Maybe? She looks at the image and then at Jampa.

"It is a Windhorse. The Windhorse is a mythical Tibetan creature that combines the power of the wind with the strength of the horse so it can take prayers from Earth to the Gods. It carries the 'wish-fulfilling jewel' on its back and brings peace, wealth, and harmony. It is time to let this go." Jampa taps the contract. "Let the Windhorse carry it away with blessings." He taps his heart. "And, before you leave, it is time to open here."

Faith closes her eyes. After a few moments, she looks at Jampa, sighs, and tears well up. "I ... um..." She takes a deep breath and touches her heart. "The... um... key to here. I think I lost it."

Jampa smiles his wrinkly, heartwarming smile. "The key to opening the heart is the same for everyone... release our expectations, our attachments, our judgments and open ourselves to our true Buddha nature."

Faith takes the binding off the contract and stamps a Windhorse on a couple of pages. Jampa takes them and places them in the bowl. He hands Faith the matches. Faith lights a page; the flames hungrily devour the legal treatise.

The image of the Windhorse seems to prance as the paper crinkles and blackens around it. Wisps of wind lift the ashes up towards the rapidly darkening clouds as Faith feeds page after stamped page into the bowl. Jampa watches Faith. His prayer beads move with practiced ease through his fingers.

That evening, back at the hotel, Jampa is standing with Faith. Jampa's prayer beads are in his hands, which is not unusual, but instead of praying with them, he is running them through his hands, feeling their weight as if savoring them.

He takes Faith's hands, places the precious, polished prayer beads into the middle of her palms, and closes her fingers around them. Her nails are still sharp and red. He can feel the shaking. Jampa looks into her face and the love that is this man radiates out.

"Use them well. I will remember you in my prayers. I will not forget you, Achala."

Faith looks from the beads in her hands up to Jampa and starts to cry. Even though she is not a demonstrative person, Faith gives Jampa a big hug and a kiss on his cheek.

"How can I ever repay you for your patience and kindness? And for these?" Faith rummages through her handbag and gets out her checkbook. Jampa gently stops her.

"Achala, kindness is free. Giving it to others is a gift to oneself." Tears are now streaming down Faith's cheeks, and she half-heartedly tries to wipe them away.

"I will make a donation to the Tibetan Children's Village on your behalf."

"As you wish."

"I would like to."

"So be it. Faith, remember ... to the well-organized mind, death is but the next great adventure."

"Sogyal Rinpoche? From *The Tibetan Book of Living and Dying?*"

"Dumbledore of Hogwarts, Harry Potter, and the Philosopher's Stone." Jampa smiles and Faith smiles with him though fresh tears rush to replace the tears that have already fallen. Jampa bows deeply and puts his hands' palms together in the Namaste position.

"Tashi Delek and great blessings for your journey, Achala."

"Tashi Delek, Jampa... my friend." Faith bows lower still and also holds her hands' palms together facing Jampa. Jampa gives Faith another of his priceless smiles, turns, and walks down the steps and into the darkness.

Faith surprises herself by racing after him. She gives him another big, long hug. Jampa just holds her and then lifts her off the ground and twirls her around at the end of the hug.

After Jampa has gone, Faith walks back to the Chonor House lobby entrance and stares after him; a lonely tear runs unbidden down her cheek. When she comes out of her reverie, she notices that the Manager is standing next to her; he is also looking at where Jampa had been.

"He is a remarkable man. Though he would deny it, he is a holy man. The Lamas and Rinpoches all know this which is why they always welcome his visits." The Manager pauses and then continues. "You would never guess that in Tibet his wife and children were killed in front of his eyes. He was beaten and tortured and spent 10 years in a Chinese hard labor camp before he escaped to Nepal, more dead than alive. Yet he has no hatred or bitterness. He even teaches Mandarin at the Tibetan Children's Village."

Faith nods her head in agreement. She is surprised but, also not surprised. There was a profound depth to Jampa. He was a reassuring presence that she would deeply miss. The mystery of Jampa's damaged hands was solved; they were the result of more than just hard work.

"Love and compassion are necessities not luxuries. Without them humanity cannot survive."
~ Dalai Lama

Chapter 21

Tenzin walks down the streets of McLeod Ganj holding her prayer beads, they feel amazing. She stops to watch a colorful butterfly flutter in front of her. It finally lands on a string of prayer flags and is joined by another butterfly. Where had they come from? They take off, dance, and finally fly away together.

Faith is at a street stand looking for a present to bring back for David. Whilst she felt betrayed when he had left, Faith could now understand how he was feeling, and he was a friend that she had not always treated well. OK, she had treated him like crap.

Faith looks up from perusing merchandise and notices a nun who looks like Tenzin walking ahead of her. Immediately Faith starts to try to catch up to her and even though she has had no alcohol, her steps follow a slightly drunken path forward.

An old woman approaches Tenzin and whilst she is short and a little hunched, her smile still retains the vigor of youth. Tenzin holds her hands, and they touch foreheads.

Just as Faith is about to catch up to Tenzin, she stumbles into a heavily laden bicycle and is knocked to the ground. Tenzin turns towards the commotion and sees Faith dazed, on her back. A group of people starts to gather around her.

Tenzin moves to Faith and crouches next to her. She looks up at the people standing around. "Please, someone, some water."

Faith starts to sit up. Tenzin helps her and then places a glass of water to her lips. Faith takes a small drink and opens her eyes slowly. Tenzin comes in and out of focus. Some of the bystanders help get Faith to her feet. Leaning on Tenzin, Faith makes it to a chair in a nearby cafe. Faith sips at her water and stares at Tenzin. It is hard for Faith to find words but finally, she does.

"Thank you... and please don't go. I would really like to talk with you. Tea?" Tenzin hesitates, she had so much to do but there is something in the way that this woman was looking at her, something in her voice.

"Sure, a tea would be lovely. You don't look very well."

"I'm dying" replies Faith.

"We're all dying."

"Yeah, so I hear."

They sit for a moment, watching the street, the rickshaws, the monkeys, and the fluttering prayer flags. Faith looks at Tenzin closely, she can see that one of Tenzin's eyes is dark brown and the other one is blue. Tenzin is used to people gawking at her eyes, but it doesn't mean she likes it.

Satisfied with her inspection, Faith continues, "It's weird. I know we have met a couple of times now, albeit briefly, but I... I feel like I know you." The waiter arrives and they order tea and Faith also orders some Indian sweets.

They sit in companionable silence for a short while. Unconsciously Faith's hand touches the side of her eye as she asks, "Were you ever teased much about your eyes?"

"Yes." Tenzin takes a sip of tea before she continues, "And worse."

Faith pulls the skin beneath her right eye down and with a practiced movement of her index finger removes a darkly tinted contact lens. The brown semi-circle is poised like a very small trophy on the end of her finger. She looks up at Tenzin.

"It is purely cosmetic. I only ever wear one lens." Remarkably, Faith also has different colored eyes. That is unusual, but what is exceptional is that they are, in fact, the exact opposite of Tenzin's. Faith's right eye is blue, and her left eye is brown.

Faith smiles at Tenzin. It is a rueful smile. Tenzin is suddenly looking at Faith in an entirely new way. Faith confides with Tenzin, "Sister, I know how you feel. *Heterochromia iridium,* different colored eyes, is a rare condition in humans. It has nothing to do with Satan and everything to do with genetics."

Tenzin is still surprised. They look at each other and then at the same time, they say, "I've always loved David Bowie!" and they laugh. David Bowie, with one green eye and one blue eye, is perhaps the most famous person with *heterochromia iridium*. Other famous people include Jane Seymour, Dan Akroyd, Christopher Walken, and Alexander the Great. Both Faith and Tenzin had thoroughly researched their condition and were aware of its uniqueness and that that uniqueness was rarely celebrated.

Time passes quickly and before long the waiter returns with a fresh pot of tea. Faith's contact lens is drying out on the table. She has not replaced it.

"So, you are going on retreat. How long for? Three days? A week?"

Tenzin laughs and clasps her hands together. "Oh, no, no, no. This time I will be in retreat for three months, three weeks, three days, and three hours. This will be my second retreat..." She gives a happy sigh. "I am inspired by Tenzin Palmo: She spent 12 years in retreat. I want to do that. I think that solitary retreat is my path in this life."

Even though Faith's jaw is on the table she has retained the power of speech. "But what do you do?"

"Do? I meditate, meditate, and then after a break, I meditate, do a little yoga but ..." Tenzin leans forward in a confidential manner and whispers. "There is nowhere to hide in a cave ... from yourself."

"But don't you get lonely?"

"I have been lonely in large cities with lots of people ..."

Faith interrupts, "Amen to that!"

"But never in retreat."

"And are you actually happy being a nun? With... well, nothing?"

"Oh, very happy. I have no possessions to worry about, and you?"

Faith closes her eyes. Without meaning to, her face screws up in pain.

"Happy?... no."

Tenzin does not respond immediately. Gently she says, "Achala, happiness is a choice you make every moment of every day. External circumstances are small compared to the suffering our minds create."

Faith is quiet for a short while. They sip their tea as the sun breaks out from behind the clouds. Faith is now bathed in sunlight. Her hands are quivering and so is her voice. "There are some things... some things that can happen to children that can steal their happiness for a lifetime... maybe more."

Tenzin reaches across the table, takes Faith's hands in hers and just holds them. The sun has disappeared again behind high dark clouds that are building up around the mountain peaks.

"Achala, forgiveness, compassion, and love - these are the remedies for even the most terrible things."

Faith's head is down. She is trembling. When she looks up she is crying. Tenzin takes a packet of tissues from a pocket somewhere within her robes and gives one to Faith. As Faith reaches forward Tenzin looks at the watch on her wrist and she gasps. She quickly finishes her tea.

"Thank you for the tea. Blessings for your journey, my sister."

"Thank you and thank you for helping me, for listening. Will I ever see you again?"

"I don't think so. I leave soon for retreat; it is remote and there is much to prepare. Thank you anyway."

Faith dabs again at her eye which wipes away the last of her foundation make-up. A blotch of white skin under her eye is revealed. Faith gives Tenzin a business card. She takes a moment to read Faith's card. Obviously, Tenzin does not have one to reciprocate with, though she pats her robes in jest as if looking for one.

Faith did not seem like the huggy type so instead; Tenzin puts her hand out to shake. As they shake, she gives a verbal business card, "Tenzin, title - Nun, no fixed address." As she is looking at Faith, she notices the white patch.

"Faith you might want to tidy up under your eye, there's some cream there or something."

Faith knows what Tenzin is talking about. She takes out a compact mirror and inspects her face. "Oh... that... Imagine as a little girl, I had these weird eyes and a tear-shaped birthmark on my face. In a way, I have been a marked woman all my life and I hated it. I had this mark blasted off with a laser as soon as I had the money, but the skin has never fully recovered." Faith gives a forced little laugh. "I was born in the year of the dragon, so my older brother used to call it my dragon tear but..." She looks up at Tenzin, "Other people were not so... kind."

"Different eyes and a birthmark on your face... sounds tough."

Faith nods in agreement. Tenzin looks into the café. There is a large mirror opposite them. Faith looks up too. The sun somehow smuggles out a few lonely beams before it is overwhelmed by the coming storm. Opposite-colored eyes peer at each other in the mirror. The mirror. Tenzin touches her eyes and as she looks at Faith, it suddenly hits her. Her eyes were the mirror image of Faith's. The prophecy. 'Found by her mirror.' No. No way. No?

Faith picks up her handbag and leaves a generous tip on the table. "Normally my birthmark becomes noticeable only when I'm under severe stress and I run out of make-up. Apparently, dying qualifies as severe stress." Faith gives a little snort as she picks up her shawl from the back of the chair. Tenzin's head is swimming, and she is a long way from a pool. Could this be?

She wanted to pretend that she had never met Faith, ignore her eyes but Tenzin had been at the sacred lake, she had heard the prophecy firsthand and she would never forget it. Oh, fudge.

Oblivious to Tenzin's sudden turmoil, Faith continues talking, "Actually, I need to start packing myself. I am going home." She smiles, it is a sad smile.

"Thank you, Tenzin. It is funny how we have the same different colored eyes but reversed. What a coincidence, huh? Anyway, thank you for looking after me, Tashi Delek."

"Tashi Delek, Faith. Faith, you know… maybe we will see each other again." Tenzin bows and is gone.

*"We must be willing to let go of the life we
planned so as to have the life that is waiting for
us." ~Joseph Campbell*

Chapter 22

Torrential rain is pelting the roof of Tushita Monastery, but
the sound is mostly drowned out by the howling of the wind. A
gathering of Gurus is taking place. Every senior lama in Lhasa is
present. Spirited discussions are taking place around the room.

Traditional Tibetan debating hones knowledge and is
theatrical, accompanied by hand slapping for emphasis and it is
normally done pacing back and forth. Whilst it may look chaotic, it
is highly orchestrated, dramatic, and entertaining.

Gradually the pockets of debate around the room stop and
the room falls silent. All eyes have turned expectantly towards His
Eminence Chodrak Trungpa who now has the floor.

"The meaning of the vision, the melting of the chains of
oppression, is clear and most welcome news but the mechanism and
the timing of the vision are clouded."

There is general consent. His Eminence holds the seal from
the Abbot of Sera Monastery in his palm. There is no wooden
handle. To smuggle it out Tenzin had removed the seal from its
ornate shaft. No one asked how she had managed to smuggle it out
and she did not venture any details though she blushed furiously
any time it was mentioned.

"When the incarnation of the Dakini marked by the tear of
the dragon is found by her mirror, the chains of the dragon will melt
from the land of snows."

An old lama speaks, "A vision of a free Tibet, the melting of the chains of the dragon." He pauses before he continues. "I have been repeating it as a mantra. Every time I hear it, it brings me great joy. But what is a tear of the dragon? A gem or a pearl? And if she is to be found next to her mirror, what kind of mirror? Silver? Gold? A calm lake? Where is it? So many questions."

There is a murmuring of agreement. Chodrak Trungpa holds his hand up for quiet. "It is confusing, but then the meaning of Padmasambhava's prophecy in the 8th century was confusing, too, for nearly a thousand years."

Tobgyal Rinpoche is one of the oldest men present. He recites the ancient prophecy though they all know it by heart.

"When the iron bird flies in the sky and horses run on wheels, the Tibetan people will be scattered across the earth, and the Buddha dharma will spread to the land of the red-faced man."

Tobgyal Rinpoche continues... "Iron birds and horses on wheels, airplanes and trains. In the 8th century, these things had not even been imagined." He suddenly smiles, and his wrinkly face lights up.

"We are due an uplifting prophecy, but we cannot wait many years let alone a thousand years for this to come true. The chains of the dragon grow ever tighter."

It has been a long and fruitless night. Whilst it was only 9:00 PM most of the men gathered started their morning meditation practices by 5:00 AM, at the latest.

Yeshe Trichen Rinpoche can see the tiredness, but also the excitement about the prophecy. "We have been over and over this, so unless anyone has any new thoughts? We will meet again..."

Rinpoche stops as a door creaks loudly as it opens, and a breathless Tenzin is escorted into the room. She walks up to her Rinpoche who, after a moment, calls His Eminence Chodrak Trungpa over. They move to one side of the room and listen as Tenzin whispers to them. Tenzin's obvious excitement infuses the room.

Finally, Yeshe Trichen turns to address the gathering. He looks surprised, confused, and delighted all at once.

"There is a possibility that Tenzin may have found the tear of the dragon and..." He looks at Tenzin and smiles. "The mirror too. Tenzin will explain."

Tenzin blushes deeply. When she faces the room, she freezes. Whilst speech eludes her, her peripheral circulation keeps the blush topped up. Rinpoche can see her distress and comes to her rescue.

"I will explain what we have just learned as best I can, with support from Ani-La." It doesn't take very long to explain what Tenzin had come to tell everyone. It had sounded better in Tenzin's head than when it was explained by Rinpoche. Two women with different colored eyes were going to unlock the Chinese chains of oppression that were strangling Tibet?

An elder, Lama Dondrup, finally speaks, "How could this Western woman be the key to freeing Tibet? Just because her brother called her birthmark a dragon tear?"

From within the crowd, a voice calls out, "Perhaps the prophecy is a trick?"

"And who would play such a trick? The Chinese Government starting a prophecy of a free Tibet? Hmmm?" It is hard to see who responded, but a gentle ripple of laughter runs through the room.

Lama Dondrup continues, "Perhaps the vision speaks of a different woman? This American, Faith McCormack, is a vessel?"

Lama Dorje, who is even older than Lama Dondrup, replies. "I have met this woman and, well... I did not think to myself ahh, here is a Dakini, here is the female embodiment of enlightened energy."

Lama Dondrup chuckles to himself, "She offered me $35 million dollars to find her ..."

Lama Dorje pretends to be outraged, "What? She only offered me $28 million."

"Yes, but you are very old and have no teeth." Lama Dondrup gives a huge smile. The few teeth he has left are lonely. Lama Dorje smiles, too, and he only has a molar or two more than his friend.

"I want to believe it but ..." Lama Dorje does not finish his sentence; he leaves it hanging in the room before His Eminence steps in.

"No, you only want to believe some of it."

"It is not just that it is a Dakini, a woman. But this woman?"

This comment sparks some spirited debate. Tibetan Buddhism has been highly patriarchal for a long time. Nuns were not permitted access to some of the higher teachings because of their gender.

Somewhere along the past thousand years, men had agreed that it was not possible to reach enlightenment in a female body. Buddha never said this, and this old misconception has been publicly and frequently dispelled by His Holiness the 14th Dalai Lama over the past decade, but old ways of thinking can take time to change. To be fair to the men present, if Faith was a Dakini she wore a very convincing disguise of profound unenlightened self-interest.

"Hmmm." Yeshe Trichen Rinpoche contemplates before he speaks. "I agree that it is difficult to accept that this... rather unique spirit could somehow be the Dakini that is the key to an unchained Tibet, but I also ask you this, has anyone here got a better alternative?"

The debate could continue spiraling but it is late and His Eminence steps in. "I propose that we ask the Nechung Oracle to confirm both the vision and this new interpretation."

This was not something to be requested lightly. The Nechung Oracle, or the State Oracle of Tibet, comes from an ancient lineage of ordained monks who channel Dorje Drakden, one of the principal protector deities of the Dalai Lamas and Tibet. Through ritual, dance, mudras, and mantras the Oracle is invoked and temporarily possesses the body of the host or medium.

"No act of kindness, no matter how small, is ever wasted." ~ Aesop

Chapter 23

Faith looks out of the back window of the taxi. Chonor House disappears behind curtains of pelting rain. It is early but it is already getting dark. She sighs heavily before she turns around. The driver puts the windshield wipers up to the fastest speed, but they are not able to keep up with the volume of water dropping from the sky. Their speed slows to a crawl.

Faith does not have nearly as much luggage as when she arrived. The Manager of the hotel had presented Faith with a book on Tibet as a parting gift. She opens the book to a random page. A figure wearing an elaborate costume consisting of a large ornate headdress, layers of colorful robes, and a round mirror on his chest is being held up by supporting monks. It is a photo of the Nechung Oracle, the State Oracle of Tibet.

After hours of ritual, the Nechung Oracle enters a trance state. A sheet of parchment with the vision written on it is given to him and his body goes rigid. After some time, he beckons to one of the specially trained attendant monks to approach him. The Oracle whispers to the monk. It takes a great deal of effort. As soon as he is finished talking, the Oracle collapses exhausted, and the parchment falls from his fingers.

Monks rush to the Oracle to remove the heavy headpiece. After they make him more comfortable, they carry his inert form from the room. He will require days to recover from the experience.

The fierce storm thundering outside drowns out all other sounds.

In the guest lounge of the Chonor Hotel, candles and a roaring fire in the fireplace light up three soggy lamas. Steam is coming from their robes and there are puddles of water on the floor where they are standing. The storm is still raging. There is no power. Finally, the Manager, with Faith on his arm, enters the room. Faith is weak and she has no contact lenses in or makeup on. Interestingly her birthmark is clearly visible.

The Manager escorts Faith to a chair near the fire before he bows to the lamas and leaves. Faith looks like she has just been woken up. She is dozy but also curious. She bows to the lamas who bow back. They all stare at her different-colored eyes.

Yeshe Trichen Rinpoche speaks first. "Achala, we were afraid you had left."

"I did leave but the airport is closed because of ..." They can all hear the storm and as if on cue, it surges fiercely for a moment before subsiding.

The lamas all look at each other; they shuffle their feet around. They are all uncharacteristically agitated. His Eminence Chodrak Trungpa and Lama Dorje both look at Rinpoche.

Rinpoche steps well into Faith's personal space. He peers intently at her birthmark. It is shaped like a tear drop. Faith is not comfortable with this close scrutiny, but she remains still. Finally, with a little grunt of satisfaction, Rinpoche steps back.

"We have reconsidered. We agree to find your next incarnation."

Faith is surprised. She takes a moment to consider this change of attitude and allows herself a small, smug smile. It looks a lot like a shark grinning at a tuna.

"Time to deal, right? Well, you have waited a bit long; the original offer is now down to $18 million dollars."

"No."

"OK, look, I'll make it $20 million but that is my final offer."

"No."

"OK ... fine, $22 million dollars, take it or leave it."

"We will leave it, the money. We will accept no payment for this." He exhales loudly, hesitates - and then makes a decision.

"There is a prophecy. You understand about prophecies?"

Faith nods her head even though her knowledge of prophecies was entirely limited to manipulating the financial markets.

Slowly, Rinpoche continues, "True prophecies are often cryptic, and difficult to interpret. Some so-called prophecies are just oft-repeated 'sayings' or wishful thinking... similar in many ways to yak dust. We believe that an authentic vision has recently come out of Tibet. This prophecy is... very important and... well, we believe that your next incarnation will play a role in melting the Chinese chains of oppression that are destroying the Tibetan way of life. Of course, it is vital to us that this prophecy is fulfilled."

Faith digests this and cannot believe her luck. Finally! That doesn't stop her from looking craftily at them.

"Right then - OK. Good... great... a prophecy. I like it... Hmmm, well, excellent, it looks like we've got ourselves a deal then."

The lamas are relieved. The tension that was in the room finished drying itself by the fire and leaves.

"So... which one of you is going to lead the search for me?"

The lamas all look at Rinpoche. He carefully wraps and rewraps his prayer beads around his wrist. Eventually, he replies.

"It must be a nun."

"A woman? No way! I want a man. I want one of you to lead the search; or no deal." Faith points at each person in turn, though her finger passes over Lama Dorje rather quickly.

"You and this special nun are parts of the one prophecy. You have met her already, Tenzin, she is your mirror. For the prophecy to be fulfilled, for Tibet to be freed, she is the one who must find you."

Faith is torn, Tenzin was nice, very nice, but she was just a nun, and they were talking about the person who was going to inherit her fortune. "I'm sorry. If that is the case, then the deal is off!"

The lamas are surprised at this proclamation. They stand around but it seems there is nothing more they can do. Each of them had already 'negotiated' with Faith. Her stubbornness was one of her more attractive traits, though, to be fair, in the attractive traits department there was not a lot to choose from. As they unwillingly turn to leave, Rinpoche gives Faith a little bow.

"It seems we were wrong about you being part of this prophecy, so sorry to have troubled you. Tashi Delek!"

Faith didn't expect this; she wanted her way, not no way. "WAIT! OK... OK, just as long as you, Rinpoche, promise to help!"

Rinpoche smiles and says, "Of course... we could have just waited until you were dead, but it is much better this way."

Faith is shocked by this statement, and it takes her aback. These lamas were compassionate, they were not fools.

Tenzin has almost finished packing up her room in the monastery. It did not take long. The bed is stripped. The shelves are empty. She wraps the final item from her altar and carefully places it in her bag. She is humming a happy mantra when there is a knock at the door.

"Please tell the driver I'll only be a minute."

Tenzin zips up her bag. She looks around once. She smiles and bows to the room. There is another knock.

"Thank you room. Good-bye."

Tenzin opens the door and is startled to find Yeshe Trichen Rinpoche poised to knock again. Tenzin starts to do prostrations, but Rinpoche indicates for her not to.

"Rinpoche, this is a great surprise. I didn't expect to see you again for at least a month." Rinpoche plays with his prayer beads. He smiles somewhat sheepishly and stands there struggling to find the right words.

"Jetsunma, this is ... difficult. It is important that your retreat is delayed – once again, maybe for some time. The prophecy…"

Rinpoche and Tenzin walk in silence on the grounds of the nunnery. They stop at a white stupa that has a forest of prayer flags radiating from it. Tenzin is incredibly disappointed. She had prepared for years for her retreat.

The first delay, the opportunity to go to Tibet had been an amazing once-in-a-lifetime opportunity that had not quite gone the way she had thought it would. Solitary confinement was not the same as being on retreat. To put it off again? She was just so ready, so attached to completing it; in as unattached a way as her Buddhist training could muster. If she could just do her retreat, then she would feel prepared to help with the vision.

Tenzin was so busy feeling sorry for herself that she was finding it difficult to concentrate on what Rinpoche was saying.

"This woman's mind is a maelstrom of attachment, anger, greed, and regret." Rinpoche pauses to make sure that Tenzin is with him. "If she dies without being able to control her mind, it will be… impossible… almost impossible to find her reincarnation, providing, of course, that she is reborn as a human."

"So, Rinpoche, let me see if I have got this right… you are saying - that the future of a free Tibet rests on how well I, the mirror, can teach her to become a Dakini and prepare her mind for her death?"

Rinpoche smiles and nods his head in agreement. The nodding is perhaps a little too vigorous. His prayer beads click swiftly through his fingers.

Tenzin continues, "Rinpoche, you know I am very happy for Tibet, but I just thought I would have time to recover from my Tibetan 'adventure'... and I will be so much better prepared for this if I can just... and I am so happy for Tibet." Tenzin falters as she realizes that she is arguing futilely with herself. This new information was hard to process.

Tenzin straightens out one of the prayer flags that surround an ornate stupa. "I... I owe... if I hadn't found you and Buddhism, I would... I would have killed myself. Tibet has given so much to me... to this world. I, I owe my life to Tibet."

"Ani-La, you owe nothing. It is all Karma. There is no debt." They stare at each other. Reluctantly, Tenzin nods.

"Then it is agreed. It is time for you to share your wisdom and compassion."

"But Rinpoche, I don't know enough to teach anyone. I'm just a student myself."

Rinpoche laughs. "I, too, am just a student, and Ani-La, only a few students have had the profound privilege of learning from my old master, Abbot Chodha in Tibet."

He sighs. It would have been wonderful to have seen his old teacher one last time. They stop walking and look at the mountains.

"Tenzin, this will be very difficult. Even as you teach Faith to control her mind, her brain will continue to degenerate. This is... most unusual."

Rinpoche wraps his prayer beads back around his wrist. "I will visit regularly. Of course, I will join you for the passing over and assist you as Faith journeys through the Bardo." Tenzin nods her head. She musters up some bravado, but it is not congruent with how she is feeling.

"Lucky I'm already packed. Where am I off to?"

Rinpoche watches Tenzin's face carefully. "Chicago." Tenzin's face falls: Rinpoche knows that Chicago is the last place in the world that Tenzin wants to go to. Karma.

Tenzin lets out a sigh so loud that if she had been on a mountain, it could have triggered an avalanche. The clouds look like big fluffy cotton wool balls that have been stuck on the peaks of the Himalayas by a busy child. Shit!

*"Blessed are the Fundamentalists, for they shall
inhibit the earth." ~ Unknown*

Chapter 24

A limousine drives through the streets of Chicago as a cloud of steam snakes up from one of the sewer grates. The traffic is as heavy as the rain. On the sidewalk, a pedestrian accidentally bumps someone and gets the finger. The gesture might be a good Samaritan forcefully suggesting a prostate check to the stumbling man blinded by the rain, but probably not.

Car horns honk loudly and a police siren wails in the distance. The sounds of the big city are muffled by the drumbeat of the rain on the roof of the vehicle. Tenzin looks intently out of the front window as she drives impatiently from the back seat. She points to an intersection and shakes her head as they pass it.

"Hey driver, if we are going to Lakeside Drive you should have gone left!"

Faith looks sharply at her. "What?"

"I lived here. Pre-nun times."

Tenzin writes on her knuckles with a pen. The phone in the limo rings. Faith answers it. "Yes, David, uh-huh... great, and when will all the assets be transferred? Uh-huh, OK - so, not until then? Right. Nope, no. I haven't asked her yet."

Faith looks at Tenzin who has finished her skin scribing and is looking out of the windscreen again. Faith's self-satisfied smile is irritating. Outside the vehicle, chaos continues to reign.

"She'll be a trustee if I tell her to. Yup, no problem. OK. Ciao." Tenzin stares at Faith, at her arrogance. They stop at a red traffic light.

"Ohhhhhh!"

Tenzin follows her inarticulate outburst by opening her door and jumping out of the vehicle. Faith tries to stop her, but she is way too late. Tenzin opens the driver's door and gestures to the driver to scoot over. The driver has a plump face. He is wearing black sunglasses and is dressed in a black suit with a white T-shirt. The driver stares at the nun. Tenzin's intensity doesn't physically move him, but it helps him swiftly shift his ass over to the passenger seat.

Tenzin takes over the steering wheel; she also grabs a spare pair of sunglasses and puts them on. As Tenzin grips the wheel, the writing on the back of her hands is visible. The letters T-E-N-Z-I-N are written across her knuckles.

Tenzin revs the big engine and smokes up the tires as she accelerates. The limo goes into a controlled slide as it takes a right-hand turn. The driver is enjoying herself - Faith, not so much.

A greenish Faith opens her apartment door and escorts Tenzin into her penthouse. She gesticulates with a wide sweep of her arms. A wide sweep is required because the lavish apartment is so large. The decor is tasteful but designed to impress rather than to be comfortable or homey.

"Well? What do you think?"

"Hmmm. Given it's the Eastside, I thought it would be tacky and pretentious, but it's not that tacky."

An uncomfortable silence follows. It was not the 'ooh' or 'ah' response that Faith had been fishing for. As they wait for the luggage to be brought up, Faith attempts small talk.

"So, when were you in Chicago?"

"A lifetime ago." Sometimes small talk begets small talk.

"Oh, and when did you leave?"

Tenzin has spotted the Picasso. "Is that... an original?"

Faith insists that they celebrate their arrival in Chicago with lunch. Tenzin would rather set up her altar and meditate, but she is also hungry and there is no food in the apartment.

The Chauffeur is relieved when he finally arrives in front of the restaurant. He wasn't sure what was going on with his passengers but the atmosphere in the cab had been frosty.

Fortunately, the rain has finally stopped. He holds the door open for Faith and Tenzin who alight onto the red carpet of Chez Jacques, a three Michelin-star restaurant that was booked out months in advance. It was normally impossible to get a table, but then Faith was hardly normal, and her tips were worth bending rules for.

A few doors down from the restaurant a homeless man is begging. He is invisible to Faith. Her nose wrinkles nonetheless and she stumbles on the curb. Tenzin notices the man but focuses on helping Faith to the entrance.

Henri, the maitre d' seats Faith and Tenzin at a window table. Tenzin can just barely see the homeless man from where she is sitting. She studies the menu, frowning.

"Hmmm, pricey."

"Ohhh don't even think about it. I'm buying. Anything you want. I want you to really enjoy being back in Chicago."

Tenzin looks up from the menu; she can't see the homeless man anymore. She looks over to Faith. "Anything?"

Grandly, Faith replies, "Anything."

Tenzin looks intently at the menu; her lips move as she does some mental arithmetic. "Can I have 100 dollars?"

Puzzled, Faith looks up at Tenzin. She takes out a $100 note and gives it to her.

"Thank you. Be back in just a minute." Tenzin gets up and makes her way out the front door.

Many minutes later, an out of breath Tenzin returns and sits down. Henri finishes taking Faith's order as Tenzin settles in her chair. Faith had quickly tired of waiting.

"*Tres bien, Madam*, and I must say your 'air is looking particularly red tonight."

"*Merci* Henri, you are too kind." Henri turns his attention to Tenzin.

"And now for you, Madam?" Tenzin closes her menu and hands it back to Henri.

"Just a hot water for me, *s'il vous plait*, with some honey in it and a touch of lemon juice." Seeing his confused look at this unusual request she explains. "I'm fasting."

"Of course, *Mademoiselle*."

Faith is surprised and that surprise morphs into surliness. Henri gives Tenzin an amused look. Faith takes her time eating; Tenzin sips her water bellicosely and somewhat contrarily murmurs prayers using her well-worn prayer beads. The restaurant is warm, but their table is not.

The limousine is waiting for them as they leave the restaurant. Faith walks with difficulty but she refuses any help from Tenzin. As they approach the vehicle, the driver opens the door for them, and the homeless man walks over. Faith darts into the limo. The driver indicates that the man should clear off, but Tenzin walks up to him.

The grateful man addresses Tenzin, "Thank you, sister, thank you."

Tenzin shakes his hand, "Food. You promised."

"You have my word."

At Faith's insistence, the driver beeps the horn a couple of times. Whilst he didn't like doing it, he wanted to keep his job.

If the temperature in the restaurant was chilly, it is arctic in the back of the limo. Faith is livid. They have only driven a short way before Faith issues a command.

"Stop the car."

The limo stops and a furious Faith gets out and moves into the front passenger seat. The barrier between the front seats and the back seats slides up with a quiet hum and a surprisingly loud click.

*"Resentment is like taking poison and hoping the
other person dies." ~ Unknown*

Chapter 25

Tenzin unpacks her single small bag. Her bedroom is the 'guest' room of Faith's penthouse, though technically, it was a storage room, as it had never accommodated a 'guest.'

Faith's suitcases are in the lounge room. The housekeeper would unpack for her tomorrow.

Reverently Tenzin takes out her photo of the Dalai Lama, followed by one of Yeshe Trichen Rinpoche and one of Rinpoche's teachers, Khenchen Chodha. They are placed carefully on the surface of the dresser that she has just cleared of... stuff.

Tenzin notices Faith staring malevolently at her from the doorway as she puts her two spare saffron robes away. Finally, she unpacks her plain, white, grandmotherly underwear. Tenzin looks around the room frowning. Compared to her austere room in the monastery it is extremely cluttered.

"How dare you embarrass me?"

Tenzin ignores Faith and picks up a chair. She carries it to the door, but Faith is barring her way.

"How dare you spoil my celebration?" Tenzin puts the chair down and looks at Faith.

"You were celebrating getting your own selfish way. I celebrated by giving a hungry, dispirited man a kind word and money for food."

"You gave a drunk money for alcohol. You may have killed him. Well done. Verrrry compassionate."

"How do you know? That's just an excuse to pretend he wasn't there. What do you know of him, of poverty?" Tenzin squeezes past Faith with the chair and puts it in the spacious lounge area.

"More than you could possibly dream, sister. I went hungry, I had nothing, nothing! If I can work myself out of the deepest gutter, so can he, by just getting off his butt..."

"If you've been there, then how can you not have compassion for that man? For all the poor, the desperate?"

Faith stalks into the room and over to the open dresser. She lifts up a pair of Tenzin's underpants as if they were contaminated with highly infectious bad taste.

"You're kidding? Really? They still make these?" Tenzin snatches them from Faith and puts them back in her dresser which she slams shut. Tenzin continues to take furniture out of the room.

"Just what the hell are you doing?"

Tenzin ignores Faith and ejects a large, frill-edged cushion. After several more soft furnishing evictions, her room is more Zen-like, more Tenzin-like.

"There were way too many bananas in this room."

"Say what?"

"Mother Teresa said that in India she saw a man dying of starvation share a banana with another starving man. She said that here in America there is great spiritual poverty, there are people with so many bananas and they don't share any of them."

Tenzin stares at Faith who leaves in disgust. The large frill-edged cushion sails back into the room.

Faith shouts from the lounge room. "Yeah, well I like all my bananas and I like them where I put them." Tenzin immediately throws the cushion back out into the hallway.

It is dark outside. Morning was not late, but it was not early either, it was on its way and would not be hurried. Tenzin makes a perfunctory knock before she opens Faith's bedroom door and turns on the light. According to the bedside clock, it is 5:25 AM.

"Time to start your meditation training. Up you get."

Faith rolls over into the pillows and pulls the blankets over her head. From under the bedclothes comes a muffled "Gerrr offf! Get out! Sleeping."

"You want us to find your reincarnation? We need to teach you..." Tenzin yanks the quilt off Faith for emphasis, "How to control your mind for when you die."

"Later… die later." Whilst surrendering the quilt Faith has managed to keep hold of the sheets. Tenzin pulls the sheets off her too, so Faith has to get up. Tenzin looks like she is enjoying herself.

"Just before dawn is the best time of day to calm your mind."

"Get out!"

"Fine! I can still make my retreat. Which is where I would much rather be," sulks Tenzin as she storms out of the room. A very irritable Faith throws one leg out of bed.

"What a grouchy nun."

A while later the sun's first rays appear over the great lake. Tenzin sits facing Faith in front of a floor-to-ceiling window that has amazing views over Chicago. Faith sits slouching sleepily against said window.

Tenzin admonishes her. "Remember, keep your back straight! Very important."

"How long are we going to…?" Faith yawns. "Meditate for?"

"We'll start you with just…" Tenzin mutters under her breath but loud enough for Faith to hear. "Let's see, undisciplined mind, huge ego, hmmm… similar to a child but without the ability to learn as quickly," Tenzin speaks loudly, "Let's start with 180 seconds, that's three whole minutes."

Faith is outraged. "Three minutes!!! You get me up at 5:30 for three minutes of meditation!!" Faith would like to have dramatically hopped up, but instead, she struggles angrily and clumsily up.

"You are right! 180 seconds is too long for you. Let's make it 150 seconds. I bet you that you can't stop that little voice in your head for 150 consecutive seconds." Faith is not normally a gambler per se but 150 seconds, come on. Time to teach this surprisingly touchy nun a thing or two and a half.

"And when I do?"

"We start practice at 8:00 each morning instead of 5:30." Faith slides back down the wall and straightens up, smiling. Tenzin matches her smile and confidently raises it with prior knowledge. She is poised with a pair of Tibetan chimes in her hand.

"You realize, of course, that as soon as you think anything, like, 'I'm going to win' or 'I'm not thinking anything' or 'is it over yet?' or any thought at all, that you lose?" Faith looks less certain now. Of course, she didn't realize that, but it was too late to back out.

"I just focus on my breath, right?"

"On your 'in' breath, for now, eyes open, unfocused gaze, back straight, mouth slightly open, tongue behind upper teeth. Simple. Of course, worrying about getting all of those things right is classified as thinking."

Tenzin is enjoying this. Faith's eyes dart about, nervously. It was only 150 seconds, which was nothing... nothing. Faith moves her tongue away from the back of her teeth long enough to say.

"Right! I'm ready."

"You think so?"

"Yes, I think so."

The next morning a delighted Tenzin wakes Faith up again. The clock reads 5:29. Faith groans. "Oh my God... Groundhog Day. No wonder I hate that movie."

Eventually, Faith starts to get up before Tenzin can come in and wake her. Tenzin seemed to have taken a perverse pleasure in rousing her and Faith is keen to deprive her of that.

Faith had always been an early riser but that was when she was driven by unceasing work. Since the car wreck, her sleep patterns have been significantly disturbed. Getting up so early to do nothing by meditating was very different for Faith but there was also something weirdly familiar about it, a faint flutter of recognition from deep within her.

The time in India had been tough on Faith physically and mentally. She still suffered from the withdrawal of the constant endorphins that trading had given her coupled with doubt, regret, and bouts of what she thought was called 'boredom'. She was also having difficulty staying focused and her memory didn't seem as sharp as it used to be, which was scary.

Tenzin was waiting for her as usual in the morning. What was unusual was that in front of Tenzin was a large glass bowl filled with water. As Faith approaches with a quizzical expression on her face, she notices a second smaller bowl that looks like it is filled with... dirt?

Tenzin helps Faith to sit down next to her. After Faith is settled, Tenzin points to the clear bowl of water. "This is the true nature of mind. Clear, still, peaceful."

Tenzin picks up the smaller bowl and slowly pours it into the water. She picks up the bowl and swirls the mixture around. "This dirt represents the deluded thoughts that fill our minds. I'm not good enough, I need this to be happy, I deserve this, they did that to me, blah, blah, blah, blah, all the stories we tell ourselves."

114

Tenzin drops her voice to a whisper. "We could use toilet water for some people... Now watch what happens when we still our minds through meditation," She places the bowl back on the floor again. They both watch the dirt fall out of suspension and gradually the water clears.

"But the dirt is still in there."

Tenzin nods in agreement with Faith. She picks the bowl up and stirs the water. The water is dirty again.

Tenzin continues, "Practicing meditation does two things; when unhelpful thoughts arise, we can still the mind more quickly and it also means that we less frequently stir the dirt up. Does this make sense?"

Faith looks thoughtful, then she shakes her head in the negative. "My problem is too much dirt, too little water."

The Chicago coffee house is all polished metal with air-conditioning and staff that are both too cool for comfort. The kind of place that serves minute food portions artistically positioned on large plates. Even Faith's plate is clean. Tenzin has two empty plates in front of her. Faith stirs her latte which is in a thin, elegant glass. She stares into it, letting it settle. The coffee stills but remains murky.

"Meditation doesn't work for coffee, does it?"

Tenzin shakes her head. Tenzin is getting curious looks from the other patrons. A few are a bit sniffy about sharing their exclusive caffeine refuge with an obvious corporate outsider. Faith leans in conspiratorially towards Tenzin and whispers.

"So, what's the plan?"

Tenzin is puzzled, still peckish and miffed. How could they serve a stack of pancake? A 'stack' implies two pancakes as a minimum. "Uh, what plan?"

"The plan to find me. You know, my reincarnation." Faith would have done a drum roll with her fingers on the table if it was not out of keeping with the surroundings and a bit too melo dramatic. She was excited, but she tried to hide it. Faith was a wealth of contradictions.

"You know, Faith the sequel, Faith II, Faith McCormack: she's back."

Tenzin considers whether or not to vent some of her frustrations. She knows better but then presses the big red release button anyway. "Oh, well, for starters we thought we'd at least wait until you were dead before we started looking."

Faith looks like she's just been slapped. She's had it.

"What is it with you? I know you'd rather be on retreat, but you are not the same person I met in India."

Tenzin looks up at Faith and sighs. Slowly, she wipes her mouth with the serviette and gets up from the table.

"You are right. Please excuse me." Tenzin takes her jacket from the coat rack near the door and heads outside.

As Tenzin walks the streets of uptown Chicago, she gets stares from some people and is totally ignored by others. She doesn't notice or care. Tenzin is in her own world, a maroon and yellow splash against a drab grey backdrop. After walking briskly for half an hour Tenzin seems to make up her mind about something. She hails a taxi.

"Without forgiveness, there's no future." ~
Desmond Tutu

Chapter 26

Tenzin kneels next to a simple neglected grave in an overgrown, almost forgotten corner of the cemetery. The day is grey and overcast. The threatening cumulonimbus clouds carry precipitation and the promise to turn any form of precipitation into ice. Weather doesn't normally make promises but, in Chicago in winter, the promise of freezing any form of falling water is given freely. Technically Chicago should be called 'The Wind Chill City' but 'The Windy City' is less threatening to tourists.

The barely visible name engraved on the small headstone says "Sean O'Grady." Under a small Christian cross, the epitaph reads "Rest in Peace." The paucity of additional information is telling.

A small shiny statue of Buddha sits incongruously in front of the gravestone. The grave has been freshly weeded. A large collection of weeds are piled nearby. Tenzin's hands are dirty, and cold, very cold. With any luck the black around her fingers was just dirt and not the start of frostbite.

Tenzin sobs loudly as she rocks back and forth. Her prayer beads move rapidly through her fingers with practiced ease.

The pile of weeds is gone. It is almost dark. Tenzin's hands are inside her robes along with her prayer beads. As she reaches the end of her Mala, she takes a huge deep breath and exhales loudly. Tenzin places the prayer beads around her neck and wipes her eyes with the back of her hands. She rubs her palms together to try to warm them.

Finally, Tenzin stands up and bows to the gravestone. "I forgive you. Rest in peace." She turns and walks away. It has started to sleet.

A soggy, freezing Tenzin lets herself into Faith's apartment just as Mike is letting himself out. Mike gives Tenzin a charming smile and tips his head in acknowledgment. Tenzin is still desperately trying to warm her hands and feet. She finds Faith propped up on the couch in her dressing gown watching TV.

Tenzin looks back at Mike as the door closes. She asks Faith, "Boyfriend?" Faith gives Tenzin a secret, satisfied smile. "Oh, umm, that was Mike... my masseur."

"He must be good, you're glowing. You know, I could really use some body work. I am so tight; can I maybe book a session?"

Faith does a bit of quick backpedaling. "Ohhh um, he's a specialist, for my lower back, but I will find someone for you. You look like a maroon icicle. Why don't you have a hot bath while I get dinner?" Faith picks up her phone.

Tenzin's face is glowing red. The empty takeaway containers from Faith's cooking are stacked in the kitchen. They finish their meal in companionable silence. A full Faith keeps looking at Tenzin who is more serene now, more like the Tenzin she remembered meeting. Faith's curiosity gets the better of her. "So, where did you go?"

Tenzin looks up from half-heartedly chasing a green bean covered in black bean sauce around her plate. She knew how that bean felt. Tenzin was a private person; she did not talk much about herself and the past was behind her, except it hadn't been. After a pause, she responds, "The cemetery."

Faith is surprised. She searches for an appropriate response and instead says, "Oh, don't know how I missed you." Tenzin gives an exhalation that could have been a half laugh or a mini snort of derision. Thankfully, the smile that follows is indicative of the former.

"I went... I went to fully forgive someone, to finally let go of the past." Faith raises her eyebrows. Faith didn't get personal with people, but this sounded juicy. She somehow manages to keep her mouth shut and Tenzin continues.

"He was my husband, once."

"Really!"

Tenzin says nothing but she spears the bean and eats it. Faith is fascinated. "What did he do? Kick your cat?" Fluffy meows right on cue and snuggles into Tenzin's lap, looking up at her with her different-colored eyes. Tenzin hesitates while she strokes Fluffy. Fluffy encourages her by purring loudly.

"He broke my jaw once when he was sober, when he was drunk, he was worse."

"He hit you?" asks Faith.

"The beatings I could heal, the humiliation and verbal abuse left me suicidal. But he would always be sorry afterward." Fluffy licks Tenzin's fingers. "I would love a nice cup of Chai."

"Chai? What is that?"

"Tea would be fine."

Faith knows how to make tea. "Oh, sure. I'll get a pot going." She picks up the phone and promptly rings room service.

The second pot of tea is almost drained. Tenzin sets her cup down. "I have done so much practice on developing compassion, on forgiveness, that I thought I was complete with Sean. Of course, I never expected to come back here, ever. I expected to be as far away as possible in the mountains of India, or maybe Bhutan. As you noticed, coming back here... well, it brought up stuff for me."

"How can you ever forgive him? The bastard."

"I can hate what he did but I don't have to hate the person. I forgave him for me, not for him. To bring me peace. Forgiving him does not condone his behavior."

For Faith, this was something of a new experience, an honest and intimate conversation with another human being. The awareness of Tenzin's openness touches her. Gently she responds.

"I would have never guessed."

"There is so much suffering in the world. It took me a long while just to find the courage to leave him. He drank himself to an early death."

There is nothing Faith can say to that, and it makes her reflect on her own life. She and Tenzin were more mirror-like than she would have ever thought. Her abuse had happened as a child, Tenzin's as an adult.

*"The towns and countryside that the traveler sees
through a train window do not slow down the
train, nor does the train affect them. Neither
disturbs the other. This is how you should see the
thoughts that pass through your mind when you
meditate."* ~ Dilgo Khyentse Rinpoche

Chapter 27

It is early morning and Faith is in deep meditation, though the line between sleeping in an upright position and meditation can be thin. In the adjoining room, Tenzin is talking quietly on the phone.

"Yes, Rinpoche, she has been pestering me about the plan to find her reincarnation… So? So… Um… What is the plan?"

Tenzin looks over at Faith who has well and truly jumped over the line. Faith starts to lean to one side. Suddenly, her head jerks back upright. It looked very awkward, but it did not wake Faith up. After listening to the plan, a worried Tenzin asks, "Rinpoche, do we have a plan B?"

They have gone to Tenzin's favorite coffee house this time. It is one of only a few places in Chicago that she remembers fondly. It had booths with polished timber tables, comfortable couches, and bright local artist paintings on the walls. There was an area for children to play. Books for reading or swapping cover one wall. The coffee was organic Fair Trade certified, and the barista was gifted. Faith is the one that feels out of place here.

Each day was different for her. Today was not a good day. Her hands were shaking so much that it made it difficult to eat and her appetite was simply not up to the portions on her plate. The owner had welcomed Tenzin with an excited shriek when she saw her.

A waitress brings them fresh lattes and takes their plates away. Tenzin produces a large coffee table book from a bag and plops it on the coffee table. She is uncertain about how to proceed. Eventually, she gets up and moves from her side of the booth and sits next to Faith.

"The plan... well, the plan to, well, to find your incarnation is to thoroughly, and diligently, apply all the traditional Tibetan practices that have been used for centuries to find important incarnations. Yes, we are going to employ tried and trusted methodologies that include... visions..."

Tenzin opens the book to a photo of a meditating monk who is apparently having a vision. The helpful caption confirms this.

Tenzin continues, "...consulting Oracles." Tenzin flips through the book until she comes to photos of the Nechung Oracle and the Gadon Oracle. They both wear amazingly ornate costumes. Faith is not that impressed by the dress-ups. Now, if they had secured the resources of the NASDAQ-listed Oracle Corporation, that would be something.

Tenzin can sense Faith's growing impatience. "...and various divination methods." Tenzin slowly shows Faith the pages that describe various methods of divination; the use of identical dough balls each with a different possibility written on thin paper and baked inside, the use of dice, mirrors, prayer beads, and observing the flames of a butter lamp.

Tenzin explains to Faith that certain masters were adept at different divination methods, and that divination was never done for personal gain but for the relief of suffering for all beings.

Tenzin attempts to make Faith understand what a privilege it was that, for example, the mirror divination of one of Tibet's principal guardian Goddesses, Dorje Yudronma, was to be used on her behalf. Faith's jaw clenches as tightly as her mind. Tenzin continues to bat on even though Faith has taken the ball and walked off the field with it.

"We will be performing special pujas or ceremonies too." Tenzin points to a photo of the Gyuto Monks performing a puja. This does not bring Faith back into the game, so Tenzin finishes quickly.

"So much energy to support you, prayers, dreams, signs, everything. Of course, every potential candidate that we find will be tested..."

Faith can't hold back any longer. "Yes, yes, great, all great. I've read all about them, but sweetheart..." There was trouble coming if Faith was calling her sweetheart. "...Tibet only had how many people?"

"Six million Tibetans before the invasion, about five million after the Chinese invasion." Faith is surprised but she does not pause to do the maths on statistics that would stun most people into silence.

"Right, right, but if I reincarnate here, the good ol' US of A has 290 million people and cars, planes and trains. Honey, you are in charge of finding the next 'me.' All the usuals would be just dandy if we were in ancient Tibet, where people traveled by yak or by foot. I need a better plan than – 'the usual.' I want 'the plan' to include the use of some of the technology that is now available." Tenzin had had a premonition that Faith would react this way. Unfortunately, she was right and now defensive.

"But that is all that Rinpoche said."

"So?"

"So that is the end of the matter ... for now," and Tenzin nods her head trying to bring the subject to a close.

"Hell no, Tenzin! Just pick up the phone, ring him." Tenzin is shocked by this suggestion. Faith did not appear to have any appreciation for how busy and how precious Rinpoche's time was or how fortunate she had been to have met with him and all of the other masters.

"No. No, I... I couldn't possibly."

Faith would have made a terrible horse; if they had ever managed to get a bit in her mouth, she would have died rather than give it up. "Why? Does Rinpoche get angry when people question him?"

Tenzin can feel herself on firmer ground now, confidently she answers. "Oh no, no, certainly not. The opposite in fact, he encourages us to question everything. I... I just haven't really had to ... yet."

All Faith does is raise her eyebrows. She raises them so high in fact that she could be an Olympic eyebrow gymnast. Tenzin finds that the firm ground was not so firm after all. Her defense sounds hollow, even to her. To make herself feel better, she offers Faith a lame, though true, excuse.

"He is very, very, busy. We'll be fine. Really."

Fluffy is curled up in Tenzin's lap while she is sitting in front of a low table reading a Buddhist text. Faith has a book on her lap, 'Karmapa: The Politics of Reincarnation.' Faith suddenly sits up straighter. Her lips move as she reads and then rereads the same passage.

"Tenzin, it says in here that, before he died, the 7th Karmapa wrote down the location and names of the parents for his next birth. How is that possible?"

"It is said that the great masters can choose the place and time of their next incarnation. Some leave detailed letters many years before their death, others send visions, signs, and dreams that help to locate them. In some cases, it is reported that after death the corpses of masters move to face the direction in which they will be reborn. The bodies of masters may remain fresh for weeks after death. It is explained that their soul leaves their body so gently that their body does not even realize that it has gone."

Faith's logical mind automatically rejects this. "Get out of here."

Tenzin shrugs and goes back to her reading. She carefully puts one rectangular page down on the pile in front of her before picking up another one. Without looking up she says, with more than a hint of mischief, "As incredible as it may sound, every master has managed to make it past the magical three-minute mark for uninterrupted meditation."

"I'll have you know that I nearly got up to five minutes yesterday... before I checked how long I had been going for... Tenzin, maybe I'll make it easy for you, leave you an email with GPS coordinates."

Tenzin rolls her eyes so only the whites are momentarily visible. She gets up and walks into the kitchen followed closely by Fluffy. Once out of earshot, she mutters under her breath, "At the rate you're going 'honey,' we'll be doing well if we get a human rebirth." Fluffy miaows her agreement.

Judging by the light coming through the window it is well after midday. Faith is clearly no longer reading. Her eyes are anywhere but on her book. She sighs heavily then loudly slaps the book shut. Tenzin jumps at the sudden sound.

Faith stands up and stretches, "Enough. Enough! If I don't get out of this apartment, I swear I'm going to die of boredom and never come back."

Tenzin looks up at Faith. "Well, I was thinking of visiting the Dharma Center today?"

"Dharma Center?"

"Dharma refers to the teachings of the Buddha, so a Dharma Center is..."

"I know what a dharma center is! I just didn't know there was one here. ...Oh great! I was thinking of something a lot more wicked, but why not? If I'm being good, I may as well be really, really good. Build up a few Karmic credits."

"Argue for your limitations and sure enough they are yours." ~ Richard Bach

Chapter 28

The Dharma Center is housed in an unassuming building. The décor includes colorful Tibetan carpets, wall hangings, a vegetarian café, meditation room, and a library. There are posters in prominent places promoting two upcoming talks by Sonam Rinpoche. The talks are to be given in the Dharma Center's main hall which can hold over 300 people.

There are more statues and images of Buddha in the world than any other religious icon. The Dharma Center does its part in keeping Buddha number one.

For the first time since McLeod Ganj, Tenzin is not the only one walking around in saffron and yellow robes but the story of her studies, capture at a sacred site and subsequent deportation from Tibet is well known at the Centre. Indeed, the letter from the Dharma Centre's patron, Senator Tate had saved Tenzin's life.

That Tenzin had risked her life to smuggle out a prophecy that could free Tibet was still a closely guarded secret: Which was just as well. Tenzin was already a hero without anyone in Chicago knowing the full depth of what she had achieved.

Soon after they arrive, Tenzin is recognized, and news of her unexpected visit is greeted with great excitement. She is surprised and not comfortable being the center of attention, though Tenzin is touched by everyone's concern for her. In an attempt to escape the interest, she retreats to the library and becomes particularly attentive to Faith.

Faith finds Tenzin's embarrassment entertaining. Faith's trading success had eventually made her the center of attention wherever she went. She had hated it, at first. Since her accident, the fickle limelight of fame had swung onto other personalities. She had recently come to the realization that she missed her notoriety. Interesting.

Despite Faith's protests, Tenzin decides that Faith is just too sick to stay and that they need to get her home as soon as possible. Tenzin tries to slip them surreptitiously out of the Dharma Center but as they near the exit, Patty, a large, bespectacled, silver-haired woman rushes up to them.

"Tenzin! Tenzin! I'm so glad I caught you." Patty takes a moment to catch her breath. She is not very good at breath catch and it takes a shot of an inhaler before she can continue. Tenzin considers running for the door, though walking briskly would be fast enough to escape. Sensing this, Faith increases the grip on Tenzin's arm. Faith is surprisingly strong.

"Sorry, Tenzin... sorry... we have a problem, a big problem." Patty points to one of the posters. "We have just been told that Sonam Rinpoche has come down with a terrible flu and he is too sick to travel. He won't be here for tonight. We have a full house. Would you be able to fill in for him? Please? Please?"

Patty owned a big, fat Labrador dog. It was a moot point whether the dog looked like Patty or Patty looked like the dog. The fact is, Patty made her eyes get bigger, her jowls drooped, and she gave Tenzin an appealing 'begging for a speaker' look. A look that was impossible to refuse. Almost impossible.

"Ohhh, Patty... I... I'm busy and I have to look after my very sick friend. She relies on me and I'm sure you can find someone better than me. Sorry, she is... really not well." Behind Faith's back, Tenzin points at Faith and mouths "Dying."

Before Tenzin can drag Faith off, Faith chimes in, "I am feeling fine. Tenzin would be delighted to help! I'll make sure she shows up tonight."

Patty is so delighted she wags... wiggles her sizeable posterior. The look that Tenzin gives Faith is one that any vengeful deity would be proud of.

That night, as Tenzin and Faith arrive at the brightly lit Center, they notice that the big posters outside have a white rectangular strip with 'Venerable Tenzin Choedon – Recently returned from Tibet Replacing Sonam Rinpoche as the Guest Speaker.'

The main hall is beautifully decorated with thangkas and flowers. It is standing room only. Sonam Rinpoche was a popular speaker. It didn't hurt that he looked like Jackie Chan. Faith is in the front row, grinning like a Cheshire cougar.

The butterflies in Tenzin's stomach seemed to have flown her entire stomach out of her body just to make room for more butterflies. After throwing up twice, the butterflies knew she wouldn't miss her stomach for a while.

Patty's introduction just makes Tenzin more nervous, if that was possible. She would like to meet the Tenzin that Patty describes...because it doesn't sound like the Tenzin she knows. Finally, after a few announcements, Patty finishes and steps down to one side of the raised platform waiting expectantly for Tenzin to take her seat on the dais.

Tenzin is surprised to find that her legs work against her will, traitors. People who criticize deer and call them stupid animals for becoming immobilized by a car's headlights have never been blinded by a spotlight in front of a large audience. Tenzin was never disparaging about deer.

After a pause so pregnant that the audience was left hoping that Tenzin's talk could be induced, she begins, but only after checking her notes for the tenth time.

"Well, umm thank you, Patty, for that kind introduction... and ummm thank you all for, ahhh, coming out tonight. It was a, a surprise to be asked to, ummm speak. Quite a surprise." Tenzin titters nervously. If her sphincter was any tighter it would snap. "I... I... ahhh I am going to be talking about, the spirit of compassion, and... ahhh I thought we, ummm..."

After 30 excruciating minutes, Patty mercifully steps in and calls an early break. Tenzin hopes that during the break she will stop sweating so profusely and that the world will end. She finishes the glass of water on the table next to her and walks over to where Faith is leaning against a wall.

The crowd is milling around, chatting and drinking tea and munching on biscuits. An opinionated middle-aged woman, Doris, has her back to Faith so she doesn't see Tenzin's approach. She steps confidently onto her highly polished, personal soap box.

"What a pity Rinpoche couldn't make it. The nun seems nice enough ..."

One of Doris' friends watches as Tenzin quietly approaches them. She knows what her friend is going to say, and she gestures to her friend to shut up, but she is hampered by holding hot tea and a mouth full of biscuit.

"But she is a *dreadful* speaker. Owww! What? Ohhh..."

The friend resorted to the 'step on the toe of the big mouth' method of censorship. Both women are embarrassed, and they move off quickly, towards the exit.

Tenzin couldn't help but hear the comment. She gives Faith a chagrined look before saying, "I think it's going quite well, don't you? Everyone seems happy, except for those two, of course, and then there are those three over there and the 12 whispering near the cookies and, and ..."

Tenzin sighs and her shoulders crumple. She confesses to Faith, "I'm terrified up there. I've heard many people would rather die than speak in public, how very enlightened of them... us."

Faith is not enjoying this as much as she thought she would. She feels for Tenzin. Yes, she had dropped her into it but how was she supposed to know that Tenzin would be so bad? She always seemed confident. Oops.

"Tenzin, maybe it would help you if you pretend that you are speaking to just one person, focus on only one person... a friend... like me."

Tenzin looks up at Faith. She had used the 'f' word. They share a smile. It had been a tough couple of weeks for them both, friends? Maybe?

"If any more people leave, I might be."

*"Sometimes the road less traveled is less traveled
for a reason." ~ Jerry Seinfeld*

Chapter 29

Tenzin sits curled up on the couch with the phone tucked into the crook of her neck talking with Yeshe Trichen Rinpoche. Faith is in the shower.

"But Rinpoche, the only people that didn't leave were asleep. I simply can't do it. I am not a public speaker. I do not enjoy public speaking. I hate it."

Rinpoche is not accepting Tenzin's excuses. His unwelcome response is, "I understand. You can do it, have faith."

"Rinpoche, while we are on that subject, I have had Faith up to..."

Just at this moment, Faith enters the room in a bathrobe with a towel wrapped around her head. Tenzin stops talking and pretends to be listening intently to the speaker before she quickly finishes the call.

"Yes, yes totally. That sounds like a really... umm, good plan. Thank you, Rinpoche. Tashi Delek."

Faith is curious. "And?"

Tenzin squirms. Sitting in a cave would be so much simpler. "Rinpoche thinks that as well as all the traditional methods ... that it would be good for me to do talks around the country. To raise my profile, keep me moving around... as a way to help me find you or your incarnation to find me... once you are ..." Tenzin can't finish, and she avoids Faith's intense gaze.

Faith finishes the sentence for her, "Dead? Well, that's a... that's a really shit plan. Why didn't you say, "Thank you Rinpoche but can I have a plan that isn't total crap, please?" A sudden thought strikes her.

"He's never seen you speak before, has he?"

"I tried to tell him how bad I am, but I think he thinks I was just being self-deprecating."

Tenzin gives a hollow laugh. "I will meditate and pray and become a better speaker."

"Yeah ... well sister... you can pray all you want but you need action too. I tried prayer, God ... did I pray." Faith walks over to the bay window and looks out over Lake Michigan. "I prayed every night just to be left alone by my 'loving' father."

After giving Faith some space, Tenzin walks over to her. "I am so sorry." She starts to massage Faith's shoulders, but Faith shrugs her hands off angrily.

"That bastard stole my childhood; he ruined my life!"

"And he gave you life."

Faith turns to Tenzin her face a mask of pain. "I will not forgive him! Look how long it took you to forgive your husband, and you're a nun. You're supposed to be good at it."

Tenzin stands there with Faith until finally she says, "Nuns are people too, with emotions, with stuff we are dealing with. We just share a stunted sense of fashion."

Faith does not smile at the quip. She walks away and slumps onto the lounge. Tenzin follows and squats in front of Faith. Faith ignores her. Tenzin waits for some of the emotion to subside.

"Do you really want to take this anger with you into your next life?"

Faith looks furiously at Tenzin before she softens, shakes her head and bursts into tears. Faith McCormack crying, again? No one would believe it, which was fair enough, Faith couldn't believe it. She hadn't cried for a very, very long time, but since her accident... Tenzin continues softly.

"I can teach you Tonglen. In Tibetan, Tonglen means 'giving and receiving,' it is a very powerful practice in developing compassion for others... and also for ourselves."

"I don't think I can even spell compassion."

Tenzin smiles warmly, "I can help with that too."

Tenzin sits on the lounge next to Faith. Neither of them speaks for a while. Finally, Faith breaks the silence.

"Thank you, Ani-La. Thank you for putting up with me, for helping me..." Suddenly Faith sits upright; she has just had a brain wave.

"You know. Maybe I can help you with something?" It was a rhetorical question, which worried Tenzin. Not a bad worry, but Tenzin remembers that the last time Faith helped her she ended up in front of a large crowd and experienced piercing embarrassment. Tenzin digs deep, the best she can manage is the weakest of smiles.

Tenzin volunteers to step down from speaking at the Dharma Centre, hoping that anyone, maybe even one of the cleaners, would take her place but Patty insists that Tenzin get back up on the podium. Tenzin had a sneaking feeling that Yeshe Trichen Rinpoche had spoken to Patty, or Faith, or both of them. Blast.

Despite the disastrous first talk, the crowd numbers for the second talk are surprisingly strong. The Center had promoted Tenzin as the nun who had recently been deported from Tibet by the Chinese PLA which created a lot of interest. Double blast.

In the green room, which is more of a yellow pastel color, Tenzin tries to calm her mind but with 15 minutes to go, she is still more nervous and sweaty than calm. Faith is with her watching from a chair with interest and a strange glint in her eyes. As if she didn't have enough to worry about.

Just as Tenzin thinks that she is going to vomit, an elegantly dressed man sweeps dramatically into the room and starts to circle a very puzzled Tenzin. Finally, after orbiting his prey a few times he pounces, or rather because of the camp nature of his pounce it is more accurate to say that he ponces, onto Tenzin.

"Hi, I'm Randy. I'm your new publicist. Normally I don't do amateurs like you, but I like a challenge, and 'Oh, my, God,' what a challenge."

Randy puts his fingers under his chin, shakes his head and clucks his tongue and he could probably rub his tummy at the same time, too, but he doesn't. He continues to circle Tenzin.

"Tenzin, Tenzin, Tenzin. Well, we'll have to change the name for starters." He pauses for effect. "And oh that hair! God, I hate that haircut. We'll grow it out, I think a bob would look nice, don't you? Ah huh, and just yuk, the clothes. Darling, where have you been living? A cave?"

Randy plucks disdainfully at Tenzin's robe and then wipes his fingers on a kerchief that he pulls from his pocket. "Are you wearing a sack? Oh my God! It is a sack."

Randy starts to write in a notebook. He shakes his head frequently, mutters to himself, and utters an almost continuous stream of "tsk, tsk, tsk."

While Randy is distracted writing, Tenzin walks over to Faith. "Can you please tell him to get out of here? I don't want a publicist."

"If you want him to leave, Tenzin... tell him to piss off!"

Randy has finished writing; he looks up at Tenzin. "We can do something if we can make that maroon sack a lighter color, maybe a pastel? Yeah, that would work."

Tenzin's nerves are already frayed by her extreme glossophobia, her fear of public speaking. This was not helping. She appeals to Faith. "You are really good at telling people to go jump. You tell him, for me, please? Please?"

"Nothing you say could offend Randy. Just look at him."

They both look and Randy flounces over. Tenzin takes a deep breath, "Excuse me, but ah, will you ..."

"Yes, honey? Oh, I like the husky voice thing you've got going there, yeah, ah huh." Randy checks his notebook. "Can you sing or dance? It always helps with the talk show hosts. Oh, oh, oh, oh, I've got the angle - a roller derby Tibetan nun ..."

Faith nudges Tenzin and whispers, "Go on, stand up for yourself."

Randy is circling again, "OK, honey, drop the sack. I need to see what I'm working with here."

Tenzin is shocked but Randy is oblivious, he retrieves his camera from his bag.

"C'mon girl, move it, tits and ass, I need to see tits and ass."

"Stop it! Just ... just Piss Off!" Tenzin is surprised and then mortified. After a long pause, she adds, "Please."

Randy's face falls. He crumples like a three-year-old girl denied lollies and starts to weep and wail and berate himself. "Oh my God... I am so sorry. I've offended you. I'm soooo sorry; I've done it again. I'm hopeless." Randy takes a moment to regain his sobbing. "I just try too hard to get people to like me."

Tenzin is appalled at what she has done to this poor man.

Gradually, Randy's weeping turns into fits of uncontrollable laughter. Faith also laughs loudly. It is as if she is rediscovering the art of laughter.

A glut of emotions race across Tenzin's face as the penny slowly drops, outrage, then anger, and then finally she, too, starts to laugh. Randy eventually stands up and bows to Tenzin, the campiness has disappeared.

"Forgive me Achala... for my performance. I was under strict instructions, very strict instructions." Randy looks meaningfully at Faith as he says this. "I am your publicist. I am an outstanding publicist, and I am also a speaker trainer." Tenzin is rattled.

"Right. Well, thank you... Randy. But I really don't want a publicist or..."

Faith butts in. "Yeah, well I really don't want to die either, so get over it. If your talks are going to help find the next ME, then WE need help. Randy's paid until you find little my next incarnation, whether you like it or not."

Randy gives Tenzin a friendly little wave. Tenzin glares at Faith but she has no time to say anything because, in the momentary silence, they hear Patty finishing her voluminous introduction to the Venerable Tenzin Choedon which is followed by warm welcoming applause from the audience.

Tenzin didn't even have time to get nervous or finish sweating.

"The world owes you nothing. It was here first." ~
Mark Twain

Chapter 30

While Faith is asleep, Tenzin talks quietly to Rinpoche. She is trying hard to make her complaining not sound like whining. "But Rinpoche, I hate publicity. More and more I find myself longing for the peace and quiet of an isolated mountain cave."

On the other side of the world Rinpoche, a keen soccer fan, is watching a live FA Cup game. His white and blue FC Porto dragon hat clashes with the color of his saffron robes.

The crowd noise is subdued as the ball is played conservatively back and forth across the halfway line, but Rinpoche still has to speak loudly to be heard. No one shushes him. The spectators sitting nearest Rinpoche were more Rinpoche fans than soccer fans.

"Ani-La, you are longing for somewhere else to avoid being totally where you are. When you are in Chicago, be in Chicago." Rinpoche grimaces as the crowd roars then lets out a collective "oh" as a fierce right foot shot from outside the square hits the goalpost and bounces out of bounds. "When you are in the mountains be in the mountains."

It is hard for Tenzin to hear, and she can tell that Rinpoche is distracted. She had prevaricated and procrastinated and vice versa before she had finally rung her teacher.

She hated to trouble her teacher. She had racked her brain for an alternative, but there was no one else that she could confide in regarding her mission, besides Faith. She was stressed. Normally, she would never have troubled Rinpoche with such a matter, but a publicist? That was too much. She was a nun, not a movie star. It would be a distraction.

"I am sorry to have troubled you. Where are you now, Rinpoche?"

"I am in the middle of a very exciting soccer match. Tashi Delek, Ani-La." In the background, the crowd goes wild.

Faith has done the cooking again. The takeaway containers from the Indian restaurant clutter the table. Faith eats standing up directly from the container. Tenzin shakes her head.

"Faith, please sit down and eat consciously."

Faith stuffs the last of her Chicken Tikka Masala into her mouth before she sits down. She casually asks Tenzin, "Have you... you know, helped anyone... die?" It is a funny question to ask with a mouth half-full of food.

Tenzin pauses making a pot of chai tea. It was impossible to get decent takeaway chai in Chicago. The spicy smell of cardamom, cinnamon, and cloves pervades the penthouse. Faith was relieved that the stove worked. Tenzin looks across at Faith but doesn't answer. Faith swallows.

"You know what I mean, been with them when they... passed on."

Tenzin nods her head in the affirmative, but Faith wants more. "And?"

Tenzin pours the tea into a strainer on top of a large mug and repeats the process with a second cup. As she adds honey she replies. "Life gets pretty simple near the end."

"So, what is it like? When a person dies?"

Tenzin carries both mugs over to the couch and places them on the coffee table which doubles admirably as a table that also supports tea drinking. "In India, the people I have been with... their spirits separated gently from their bodies. They were at peace."

Faith thinks about this. "Right, but what about me? No one has ever accused me of being peaceful and my brain is ... going. I could even die in a coma. Will that make a difference?"

"Hmmm, yes, it is very unusual, but I can assure you of this, we will do everything we can to help you. Worrying about what may be, is a poor investment of energy."

"God, I just love it when you talk investments."

Tenzin smiles. "Our goal with the time we have left is to generate a strong, virtuous mind. What we know beyond doubt is that the better prepared you are for dying, the easier it will be to find your next incarnation. The key ingredients are meditating for focus and emptiness, Tonglen and the Phowa."

"Power?"

Tenzin laughs and walks back into the kitchen. She returns with the honey jar and adds another spoonful to her chai, followed by one more, just a little one. "Po-wa" in Tibetan means the transference of consciousness. In the end, your spirit will leave your body through your crown chakra."

Tenzin can see that Faith does not understand, so with her hands she points to the position of the seven chakra points on her body. "The chakras are energy points in the body, softening up your crown chakra makes it easier for your spirit to leave your body when it is time."

Faith has a lot to think about. Chakras? Of course, she would research chakras but talking about dying, of her actually dying, still made her stomach churn. Up to now, she had been so busy with the trust fund, with Tenzin, with research, that she had put the dying bit out of her mind. Tenzin can sense what is happening for Faith, she smiles at her.

"Good night Faith, see you at dawn."

Faith grimaces. The 'getting up early' was not all that annoying, after all, her 'normal' working day for over 20 years had started at 5:30 AM. But since her public trading life had finished, she had constantly felt tired and she wanted more sleep, craved more sleep, but sleep was also more elusive than ever. At night, in bed she was alone with her 'condition' and though she tried to hide it from Tenzin and herself it was getting worse. While she expected it, it scared her.

Trading had provided constant access to adrenalin. Fighting Chuck had given her regular doses of testosterone. She didn't miss Napoleon Brothers, good God no. She was happy... or at least less miserable but dying too, so they kind of balanced each other out. There were times when she missed the business, the action, the risk, and the satisfaction of getting it right.

What was it that niggled her so much about the early morning meditation? Faith had never liked authority; was it Tenzin telling her what to do that did it? Or was it that she was finding it so difficult to be still? The struggle to calm her mind seemed insurmountable.

There were moments when sitting next to Tenzin and meditating felt incredibly soothing, and... and familiar to her. Faith could have taken comfort from this and used it to deepen her practice. Instead, she used it to piss herself off.

Back in her room, Faith pops the lid on a bottle of sleeping tablets and takes two. She would sleep tonight.

Dawn comes too early for Faith. With the sleeping pills, whatever 'sleep' she got was not refreshing. She started nurturing a contrary mood from the moment she opened her eyes.

She is sitting next to Tenzin who is in deep 'non-sleeping' meditation. Tenzin seemed to be able to slip into the zone so easily that it irked Faith and pricked her competitive spirit.

Faith tries to meditate again, not very hard nor for too long. She knows that it is good for her and for her next her, but after a while, she starts to slowly move her arms awkwardly in different directions. Faith adds ohm-like sounds to her movements. As she intends, her activity attracts Tenzin's attention. Tenzin is not amused by having her practice interrupted by her pupil's silly antics and obvious lack of progress. She hisses at Faith.

"What are you doing?"

Faith keeps a straight face, closes her eyes, and keeps her arms moving, thumb and middle fingers touching. "Just trying to tune in to the collective unconscious. Reception this morning is lousy."

Tenzin goes bright red; she looks like she is about to slap Faith. Instead, she gets up, races to her room, and slams the door shut with a resounding bang.

Tenzin is crying. She kneels in front of her shrine. Photos of her teacher, as well as a few of her teacher's teachers look down on her. She unloads to the photo of Yeshe Trichen Rinpoche;

"I can't do it, Rinpoche! I'm so sorry!"

The image of Rinpoche stares down at her. Tenzin continues, "She's not taking my teaching seriously. I'm not the right one to do this. I'm a crap teacher and this is too important to be left to... to me!"

Tenzin lights two tea light candles. She places one in front of her Rinpoche's photo and the other one in front of a photo of the Dalai Lama. She bows her head. "My heart's wish is that Tibet is free, even if that freedom, as you have so generously proposed your Holiness, is autonomy within China and not as an independent country."

Tenzin shifts to the photo of Rinpoche. "Please help me Rinpoche. I'm afraid all the time, so afraid… if I fail as a teacher then the prophecy can't come true, and the Tibetan way of life will get buried under the weight of continued oppression."

The candles on the altar are sputtering out. Tenzin has had a long meditation and is feeling better, calmer. As she comes out of her room, she can see Faith sitting on the couch watching CNN Business on the TV. Faith turns the TV off as soon as she sees Tenzin.

"I'm sorry Tenzin. I was just messing around..." Tenzin holds up her hand and stops Faith. She sits down facing her on the couch and takes a deep breath. Tenzin picks up one of Faith's hands and holds it.

Looking Faith in the eye she says, "I'm sorry I over-reacted. You see... this is difficult for me. I am terrified that I am not a good enough teacher. If you panic as you pass over, or hold onto anger or strong attachments to, well, money then the chances of us finding your incarnation will be remote... you are supposed to be a Dakini. If I can't find you and you can't find me... There is so much resting on this."

Tenzin sits for a moment. "Faith... this prophecy is so crucial. The Tibetan people are suffering genocide. They are either refugees who still have to report to the police regularly or they are a minority in their own country where the Chinese claim of religious freedom is a cruel farce. I ... I just love the Tibetans; they are so brave and so inspiring. Despite all that has happened there is no hatred, only compassion for the Chinese people..."

Faith is moved by what Tenzin has said and comforted by her touch.

"Thank you, Tenzin, for being so honest with me. You are a very good teacher... and I am finding meditation extremely challenging, but I know that when you are with me, that I can do it. I'm sorry about being so silly this morning."

Tenzin laughs. "It was kind of funny, but I was torn between wanting to strangle you and wanting to laugh. Wanting to strangle you was winning."

Faith bows to Tenzin who bows back. "Let's have a decent lunch today but promise me, no fasting." Tenzin nods and a nod is as good as a wink to a blind horse, as the Irish say, though why the Irish say this is a mystery.

*"The Pledge of Allegiance says, 'liberty and
justice for all'. Which part of 'all' don't you
understand?" ~ Pat Schroeder*

Chapter 31

Tenzin and Faith are sitting in the back seat of the limousine.
A block from Faith's favorite restaurant, they get stopped by a red
light. On the corner of the busy intersection Pete, the homeless man
is holding a neat hand-written sign, "Veteran. Work Wanted." Pete
is still struggling, but he is clean and tidy and there is a quiet dignity
about him.

The light changes and the limo starts to glide forward. On
an impulse, Faith commands the driver, "Stop!"

Faith gets out of the limousine. She gets the shakes when
her feet hit the pavement. She has to wait for the spasm to pass. The
limo is holding up traffic and a driver behind them honks his horn
and yells abuse at her. The honking horn draws Pete's attention to
the limo. Faith walks up to him and holds out her hand.

"Hi, my name is Faith."

Pete tucks his sign under his arm, and he shakes her hand.
"Pete. I like your name."

"Thank you."

"Well… Pete, I was wondering if maybe you would like to
join my friend and me for lunch?" Pete hesitates; it is a bit odd, this
obviously wealthy woman inviting him for lunch.

His sign said work wanted, not lunch wanted. Faith indicates
the limo with her hand. The passenger window lowers smoothly
and Tenzin smiles back at Pete. It took Pete a moment to recognize

her but the robes, the eyes, and the haircut were distinctive. Pete smiles back at Tenzin.

Faith offers, "My buy, of course."

"Well, I think I can free up some space in my schedule. Sure. Why not?"

Faith looks back at Tenzin triumphantly. She also surreptitiously wipes her hand on the back of her dress.

At Chez Jacques, Faith and Tenzin sit at the same table that they sat at for Faith's celebratory dinner. It seemed a very long time ago, but it had only been a few weeks. A third setting has been added to the table. Faith is happy with herself and just in case Tenzin does not know why she tells her, "See Tenzin, I can be nice to poor people. I can share my bananas."

Tenzin stifles a smile. Henri approaches the table with Pete behind him. Henri pulls Pete's chair out for him. Pete is wearing a smart jacket; he has shaved, and his hair is wet back. After Pete sits down, Henri shakes out a napkin with a flourish and places it on Pete's lap. Pete looks up at him.

"Merci, Henri, *mille merci*."

"Monsieur, it is my pleasure."

Henri leaves the table. Pete sits still; reverently he touches the plate and the cutlery. It had been a long time since Pete had sat in a nice restaurant. It brought up memories of a different time, a different lifetime within this lifetime. A time when he had a good job, a loving family, and a house. A time before his first 'Tour' of duty. What he had seen and done was not a 'tour,' it had pulled him apart at the seams and made him question everything he knew about himself and his country.

It seemed to Pete that he had been deliberately sent into harm's way for the profit and benefit of a few large corporations. Mentally, that conclusion combined with severe PTSD had sent him over the edge. The token psychological counseling from the Department of Defense had ticked their boxes but had not helped him.

The psychologist Pete had seen knew the theory of post-traumatic stress disorder but had no physical reference for the horror that the people he was supposed to be treating had experienced. He told Pete that he was fine, but Pete knew that he wasn't. The casual way he had been cast off had sent him over the edge; and made him so angry that he wanted to kill someone. He had turned to drugs and alcohol to try to numb the fury. He had entered a fog of despair and lost everything he held dear.

Every time Pete thought he had hit rock bottom he found there was further to fall until a few weeks ago when a single act of kindness had helped him turn it around. Moisture wells in his eyes. So much can go through a person's mind so quickly. The silence doesn't last long but Faith fidgets. There was a rawness about Pete. She could sense the emotion springing up in him.

Faith breaks the silence. "We should probably order, huh?"

Pete looks up at Faith blankly; it takes him a moment to remember where he is. He gives his body a little shake and files his past in the past; it had haunted him for too long. What was done was done. This was a new day, full of new possibilities. Pete was ready to start living again. He looks across at Tenzin and smiles, a smile that starts at his toes, goes up his body, spends a long time in his heart, and finishes in his eyes. There were good people in this world too.

Henri serves them with a twinkle in his eyes. Pete's portions of *duck l'orange* and *potato au gratin* are twice the size of the portions on Faith's plate. After Henri leaves them, they look at their food and laugh which breaks the tension.

Tenzin realizes that Henri was one of the reasons why the restaurant was so popular and why Faith was such a regular. Henri brought so much more than just amazing food to each table. Henri had a grace and compassion that pervaded the stately home-turned-restaurant.

Undoubtedly it was an expensive place to eat but it was not stuffy or pretentious. Tenzin blushes briefly as she remembers how quickly and comprehensively she had judged both Faith and the restaurant the last time she had sat at the window. Rinpoche had been right. She had certainly had a lot of lessons since she left India, lessons that would not have presented themselves to her in a cave.

When Henri brings the wine to the table, Faith holds her breath. Henri fills Faith's glass and offers to fill Pete's but he declines firmly, politely. Faith had not realized that she had been holding her breath and she tried not to exhale loudly. Henri returns with bottles of Perrier mineral water for both Tenzin and Pete.

Faith looks across and watches Tenzin enjoying her meal and it makes her happy. "Not fasting I see."

Tenzin smiles and looks at Faith's plate. She had hardly touched anything, and her declining appetite was concerning Tenzin. She chides Faith. "Looks like you are." As Tenzin looks at Faith, she sees something she has not often seen; Faith seems happy.

Savoring his last mouthful just as much as he had savored his first mouthful, Pete places his knife and fork on the empty plate. He gives a satisfied sigh. "That was magnificent." Pete sips at his water and wipes his mouth with his napkin. "Better than I often imagined."

"Would you like a coffee, Pete?" Pete looks at Faith and Tenzin and their peculiarly colored eyes.

"Yes, please." Faith looks into Pete's eyes. She likes what she sees. When did she stop looking people in the eyes? Staring down opponents was different.

Over a couple of strong coffees and a selection of French pastries, Pete shares with Tenzin and Faith the story of how he came to be living on the street and how Tenzin's random act of kindness had helped pull him out of a very dark place. He tells his tale honestly, without self-pity or excuses, and with an open heart and, eventually, a full bladder. It is a rare and precious thing to be in a space where a person can share so openly.

In the silence that follows, Pete excuses himself to go to the bathroom. Both women watch him as he walks away. Faith dabs at her eyes with her napkin and looks over at Tenzin. There are tears in Tenzin's eyes.

"Pete's story is so... so sad and he shared it so... so..."

Tenzin finishes the sentence for Faith, "Generously?"

Faith nods. "I see him differently now. He is a very brave man."

Tenzin agrees, "True compassion is to see everyone differently, without having to hear their stories. A few bananas well spent."

Pete returns from the toilets. It is time to go. They were the only patrons left. Henri had made sure that they were not interrupted or hurried, but it was late. Pete pulls the chair out for Faith and then for Tenzin.

"Thank you, ladies, for the amazing meal and just... just for listening, without judging or patronizing me. I feel better. It helped. Sadly, there are a lot of veterans living on the streets. Once I am on my feet properly, I want to use my experience to help others."

Arms joined; they walk towards the exit. Faith is wondering what she can do to help Pete when Henri comes back in with their coats. Pete starts to take off the jacket, but Henri indicates for him to stop.

"*Non, Monsieur*, it is yours. *Monsieur*, if you are interested in some work, we need some help in our kitchen..."

As the limo pulls away from the curb, Tenzin's grin manages to stretch from one side of the car to the other. It is a wide car. She gives Faith a playful nudge. Faith looks out the window and ignores her. Tenzin gives her another playful nudge. Faith smiles but shrugs her off. Tenzin nudges her again.

Finally, Faith turns to Tenzin and tries to be stern, "Stop it!"

"Oh, I'm terrified, you big scary marshmallow."

Faith can't keep her stern face on, so she breaks into one of her knowing smiles.

"Well, we'll see how soft you think I am after you've had your first public speaking lesson."

Randy is frazzled. He pulls his hair. His hair is his pride and a mess, which says a lot. Faith is pleased with how things are going. She is sitting in a chair in the front row enjoying the show. She loved helping. Tenzin is cranky and flustered. The empty room is set up for a talk.

Randy berates Tenzin. "Oh, for Buddha's sake woman! Push your chest out, lift your shoulders. You look like you're trying to hide. Let's hear it one more time."

"No! I've had it! That's enough for one day."

Faith loudly clears her throat and points at her watch. "Randy, tell her that the scary marshmallow says that compassion practice is much longer and more often than speaker practice."

"Tenzin, the marshmallow says ..." Randy does not need to finish what he is saying. Tenzin sighs, stands tall, and pushes her chest out along with her tongue.

"Great! Much better! Now, remember to breathe up from your belly ... Good! Visualize everyone in the room..."

*"I didn't attend the funeral, but I sent a nice letter
saying I approved of it."* ~ *Mark Twain*

Chapter 32

Faith had been ignoring Dr. Kleinstein's calls for three
reasons: 1) the chances of him having any good news were remote;
2) he was a jerk; and 3) see reason 2. Tenzin, however, encourages
Faith to get a checkup, again and again, and again. To stop the
constant 'encouragement' Faith relents and whilst she did not want
to admit it, anything that could help her with some of her symptoms
would be welcome.

Magnetic Resonance Imaging scanners are expensive, high-
precision, high-technology instruments. If the patient moves during
a scan it can make the images impossible to read. Since Faith had
no control over her shakes, she was given a general anesthetic.

From the glass-enclosed operator's room, Tenzin and Dr.
Kleinstein watch as an inert Faith slides out of the machine. Faith
is dressed in a plain green medical gown, one more reason for her
to be sedated. Dr. Kleinstein looks at the scan results on a monitor
and shakes his head.

He turns to Tenzin who is feeling bad about pushing Faith
to surrender herself to the hospital. Tenzin is hugging her arms
close to her body. Dr. Kleinstein frowns as he asks in an accusatory
tone, "What are you doing to her?"

Tenzin's immediate reaction is guilt. She worries that
Faith's condition has gotten worse and that somehow, she is
responsible for it. She unwraps her arms and holds her hands up,
open. Before she can respond, Dr. Kleinstein blithely continues,

"Are you giving her any special Tibetan herbs? Or Medicines? Acupuncture?"

Tenzin is one breath from panic, "Why? What's the matter?"

Dimly, Dr. Kleinstein realizes that he has alarmed Tenzin. He had recently completed a hospital board-mandated course intended to reduce litigation and help him with his appalling bedside manner. He forgot everything within a week but today he was able to spot the obvious.

"Sorry, sorry, nothing's wrong. I just... well... she has Creutzfeldt - Jakob disease..." Tenzin nods her head, even Tenzin knew this. She used a calming mudra to center herself. This guy managed to put her on edge without trying and she was expecting him to say 'but' and then follow it with bad news.

"From everything I have read... and given her case history... she should be dead by now... or at least in a coma."

He points to the computer screen as if the squiggly colorful lines meant anything to Tenzin. "The disease is progressing but not as I expected." He sounds disappointed.

Tenzin is greatly relieved. She is about to tell the Doctor about the daily meditation practice, Tonglen, and the Phowa, but Kleinstein turns his back on her, frowning importantly at the puzzling MRI results.

Tenzin retained her sense of relief, but she is now annoyed. The possibility of Faith coming back for another checkup had dropped to zero.

Faith's favorite caffeine hole is crowded with business types rubbing shoulders with other business types. When a mobile phone rings, hands go to pockets faster than a gunslinger's draw. The only person who ignores the sound is Tenzin. It is her phone. To the annoyance of the majority of the patrons, Tenzin is slow to reach within her voluminous robes to answer the call.

"Yes? Dondrup? Hi! OK, when? What? Right, OK. Yes, no she's good. Thank you for the call, Tashi Delek."

As Tenzin hangs up and puts her phone away, she looks puzzled. Surreptitiously Faith rings her just to watch all the suits dive for their mobiles. Tenzin appreciates Faith's little prank.

After her fun Faith asks, "Dondrup?"

"Strange, Rinpoche just canceled all his UK teachings and is coming straight to Chicago. He'd like to see us tomorrow evening after a small talk he is giving at the Dharma Center."

146

Later that night, Tenzin helps Faith get into bed. After Faith settles, Tenzin sits on the edge of the bed. She smooths the bedspread with her hand though it doesn't need it. The material feels silky against her skin.

"You are looking very peaceful tonight, Faith."

Faith acknowledges the compliment with a tilt of her head. Peaceful. Exhausted. Potato. Potahto. She was so tired that she would be able to sleep tonight without the tablets that Kleinstein had given her. The Doctor's amazing contribution to helping her manage the shaking, the constant itching, and the difficulty in focusing, had been to prescribe her stronger sleeping tablets.

The greatest gift Kleinstein could give the world was to get very, very sick and then be treated by someone just like him. No wonder karma was such a popular belief. If Faith could work out how to sell tickets to certain karmic events, she was sure that tickets to Dr. Kleinstein's comeuppance would be a sell-out. She would be richer than even she could imagine. Not that more money would help where Faith was going.

"Tenzin?"

"Yes?"

"What will it be like? ...Dying?"

Tenzin settles herself more comfortably on the bed. She gathers her thoughts. "What I understand dying to be... is your mind leaving your physical body. In death, there is always a moment after separation when your mind exists as clear pure light. This is a great moment for spiritual liberation, but it takes practice and training for your mind to recognize this moment."

Faith is listening intently, concentrating, "That's why we are doing the Phowa practice, isn't it? So my mind doesn't panic? And race off to... other places."

Tenzin nods her head. They sit together, each lost in their thoughts. "Tenzin, will you promise to stay with me when I am... dying?"

Tenzin smiles at her friend, "I promise, and Rinpoche plans to be with us too."

They lock eyes and Faith smiles. Tenzin teases her. "So, have you finally given up on taking it all with you?"

Faith snorts, or is it a laugh? "You know, I had almost forgotten about all that. The more I contemplate death, the less important all that other 'stuff' seems." And somewhat contrarily, Faith makes a mental note to check in with David tomorrow to make sure that all the final financial arrangements are in place. Coming back to the moment she takes a deep breath and...

"Most of all... I have enjoyed... I mean ... thank you, Tenzin ... for staying with me, for being my friend... I realize that I have not had very many friends. I don't always treat people well."

Tenzin can sense Faith's openness. She picks up Faith's hand and puts it on her cheek, and then slowly she puts it back on the bed and holds it. It is a tender moment. There is no rush for either of them. Eventually, Tenzin gets up and gently tucks the covers in around Faith. She bows to Faith and turns for the door.

Faith leans up on her elbows, "Oh, one last thing."

Tenzin turns back to Faith, "Yes?"

"After I am dead, when they dress my corpse, promise me that I'll be wearing my underwear, not yours?"

They both laugh. Tenzin nods her head; they lock eyes, blue eye looking into blue eye, brown eye looking into brown until Faith closes hers, almost asleep. A smile lingers on her face.

They are due at the Dharma Center in a few hours. Tenzin is looking forward to seeing her teacher. Faith is trying to decide what to wear, and Tenzin is helping her choose. They have plenty of time and, given the size of Faith's wardrobe, that is a good thing. Whilst it is technically described as a walk-in wardrobe, it is so spacious it would be better described as a drive-in wardrobe.

Faith opens the door and comes out of it wearing a little Miss Muffet costume that had been bought by Cheryl for Faith to wear to a costume party fundraiser. Faith had refused to wear it and she had been too busy to attend the function anyway. The outfit had been forgotten but had somehow made it into the wardrobe. Tenzin shrieks in surprise and delight. Faith curtsies and grins mischievously at Tenzin. "No?"

Tenzin does not need to reply. Going from one extreme to the other, which Faith was quite good at, she exits her wardrobe again. This time Faith is wearing a navy-blue Armani pantsuit complete with dark-rimmed glasses worn down near the end of her nose. Tenzin stands to attention and salutes her. The salute turns into a thumbs down, a double thumbs down.

Faith had forgotten just how short her red mini skirt was. The shocked look from Tenzin was everything she hoped it would be. She was having fun, silly shared girl fun. She was laughing so much that she got short of breath. Her stomach muscles were getting tired, they were not used to this type of workout.

Faith was slow changing, small buttons gave her a lot of trouble and she wanted each 'display' to be a surprise for Tenzin so she would not accept any help. Just a year earlier and she would have gotten through a lot more outfits, but then the chances she would be 'wasting time' doing this a year ago were infinitesimal.

"Faith! Just pick something! This is Rinpoche not the Oscars."

Finally, Faith comes out wearing sensible smart casual slacks and a silk blouse.

"Finally! Right. Now it's my turn."

Tenzin disappears into the wardrobe. She comes out with her robes arranged cheekily over one shoulder. She has wrapped the yellow undershirt around her head as an elegant turban, a chic African look. She struts it out as if she were a top fashion model.

Faith and Tenzin both fall around laughing.

They are both dressed and ready to go meet with Rinpoche at the Dharma Center. Faith has added a touch of makeup to her eyes. Putting make-up on for different colored eyes was a bit tricky but Faith had nailed it. In a moment of craziness, she had drawn over the outline of her birthmark in an azure blue eyeliner. The mark was becoming more visible, so she had made it into a feature rather than something to be hidden.

A hand-felted saffron shawl is draped over her shoulders. It is a similar color to Tenzin's robes. They stand shoulder to shoulder and look at each other in the floor-length mirror which is near the entrance to the penthouse. They are color-coordinated, and they could be sisters. Tenzin puts her arms around Faith's shoulders.

"You look great."

Faith looks at her reflection for a long moment. She had learned how to exploit her physical appearance, but she had never been happy with how she looked. She knew some women spent a lot of time looking at themselves in mirrors. Faith had avoided mirrors except for the unavoidable applications of 'war paint,' obligatory hair grooming, and improper cleavage management. She looks herself in the eyes and agrees with Tenzin.

She holds out her hand to Tenzin, with the other hand she takes the polished walking stick from its holder next to the door. As they leave the room she says, "I'm going to miss me when I'm gone."

"If death meant just leaving the stage long enough to change costume and come back as a new character...Would you slow down? Or speed up?" ~ Chuck Palahniuk

Chapter 33

The Dharma Center was not set up for limousine drop-offs and there was no red carpet either. Faith and Tenzin get out on the opposite side of the street to the Center. It is a short walk, but Faith uses the walking stick to help her. Tenzin is at her elbow ready to assist if she is needed.

After checking for traffic, they start to cross the wide street. Tenzin can see a few people that she knows milling around the entrance to the Center and she waves. Announced by a loud squeal of tortured tires, a car careens recklessly around a corner and accelerates.

Faith and Tenzin are caught in the middle of the street. They both turn when they hear the car just in time to get blinded by the powerful halogen headlights. It happens so fast, and so unexpectedly, that they are frozen.

Instead of braking, the driver hits the other pedal and the car jumps forward. Tenzin tries to help Faith out of the way, but the car is coming too fast. There is a temporal warp, time seems to slow…

A pair of hands push a saffron-covered body out of the way of the oncoming car. Immediately after the push, the hands join together into the prayer position as if saying goodbye.

The time spell is broken by an onlooker's scream. There is an awful screech of brakes applied too hard, too late, followed by a sickening thump. The dazzling light of the headlights fade to white...

More bright lights, this time they shine dispassionately from the lamps in the intensive care operating theatre onto a sheet-covered body. The situation is tense as the medical staff urgently operate, trying to save the life of the critically injured person on the table. The beep of the heart rate monitor is irregular. A nurse wipes sweat from the surgeon's brow. Even the best that money can buy is not always enough.

High up in the observation room, Rinpoche watches the work of the highly skilled surgical team. His prayer beads click rapidly between his fingers.

In a clinical and spotlessly clean private room that smells strongly of hospital, a heavily bandaged, wired, and dripped patient lies motionless. The heart rate monitor emits a faint but reassuringly regular beep.

Yeshe Trichen Rinpoche is standing next to the bed. Shuffling stiffly and awkwardly he is joined by another concerned person. This visitor also wears saffron, but it is a shawl rather than a robe. Faith is weeping. She is comforted by Rinpoche.

A parade of doctors, nurses, and other visitors come and go. Dr. Kleinstein is not among them. There is one constant. The constant is Faith, sitting next to Tenzin's bed, leaving only for bathroom breaks. Faith had even considered skipping those by using the bedpan, buuut, she knew that Tenzin would have wanted her to piss in privacy.

A variety of visitors bring prayers, small gifts, and a few Buddhist texts for Faith to read to Tenzin. Faith maintains her vigil, nodding off in her chair at times. Wisely, the hospital does not try to impose visitor hours on Faith. The skin on the back of Faith's hand itches interminably. Finally, a kind nurse applies a bandage to stop Faith from scratching the skin bloody... bloodier.

Faith is asleep in her chair, her head dropping gradually further and further forward until finally, it snaps backward, only to restart the process. Even chiropractors do not like to watch people do this. Jampa's prayer beads are held firmly in her hands.

A second bed is wheeled into the room and positioned next to Tenzin's. This time when Faith's head flings back and she starts, her eyes open. She looks up at the orderlies.

"Thank you." The men nod and leave the room. Faith opens the suitcase that had been brought in for her and she changes into a modest pair of brand-new pajamas. Faith tries to get into the bed, but it is too high for her to clamber onto and her climbing skills have never been worse.

Eventually, a nurse comes into the room to check on Tenzin. She lowers the bed and puts the railings down. She even helps Faith get under the covers. Faith is grateful and worn out; she is asleep before her head hits the pillow.

Bright daylight shines in from the hospital room's window. Faith is sitting in a chair next to Tenzin's bed. Jampa's... no, correction, her prayer beads click slowly through her fingers. She looks terrible, like a hawk that has dived from a great height, missed its prey, and hit the ground without braking. She was unrecognizable from the woman that only yesterday had stared at her from the mirror in her penthouse.

Rinpoche opens the door and comes into the room. He checks on Tenzin then walks over to Faith and takes her hand.

"You need a break, come with me."

Faith's rebellious nature kicks in, and she wants to protest, but she also knows that Rinpoche is right. She stands up and walks out with him, leaning on him. She looks back at Tenzin as she leaves the room.

Why did the chicken schnitzel cross the plate? Because Faith was not hungry, and she was listlessly playing with her food instead of eating it. The mashed potato didn't move, but some shriveled peas jumped the plate.

They are sitting in a quiet corner of the hospital cafeteria. The smell reminds Faith of airplane food, the smell of food suffering from self-loathing. For the first time, she could relate to in-flight food, not that it did anything to help her appetite. Rinpoche is trying to get her attention.

"Faith, you are not listening to me. It is not your fault that Tenzin is in a coma. Your intention, your motivation, was to save your friend even if that left you in the path of the car, was it not?"

Glumly, Faith nods her head in the affirmative. Another pea escapes and rolls across the table hoping to reach the ground.

"But if I had done nothing, Tenzin would be fine."

"Who knows? We can only ever have control over our intentions. Your intention was pure. We cannot always control results. Much too much energy is wasted on regret."

Faith looks at Rinpoche. Her sadness was written in every new wrinkle on her face. The depth of her feelings for Tenzin is a surprise even to Faith. Rinpoche continues, "If Tenzin were here with us now, munching on a salad, or spearing escaping peas, would she blame you for the car jackknifing?"

Slowly, Faith shakes her head, no.

"What would she say to you?"

Faith smiles wryly, sheepishly. "She would probably scold me, quite nicely, for beating myself up, for not meditating and continuing with my practice."

Rinpoche continues to stare at Faith. Faith pauses for a long time. She notices that there is a third chair at their table which is empty. Faith gets lost looking at the chair. She was still in shock. She was having trouble coping and Faith didn't mind who knew it.

Blaming herself was familiar territory and it was a way that Faith had dealt with trauma in the past, a highly dysfunctional way to deal with trauma, but a way, nonetheless. Knowing that she shouldn't beat herself up didn't mean that she wouldn't give herself a hard time and ... and yet, Tenzin's advice, even in absentia, was sound.

"Faith, are you OK?"

She doesn't answer but her tears speak volumes. What is not obvious is that part of Faith's current crisis is that she is terrified of being helpless again. It was bad enough that she couldn't do anything to help herself. Now she couldn't even help her friend. She had done whatever it took to gain control over her life, and she had been highly successful, for a while anyway.

The Doctors had said there was a possibility that Tenzin could come out of the coma at any time, but their forced optimism suggested otherwise. It was serious. There were internal injuries as well as a severe concussion. Shit! There must be something she could do...

"Rinpoche, can you remind me what the prophecy says again?"

Rinpoche nods his head.

"But remember, Faith, that prophecies are not precise, they are not contracts, and they can be interpreted in many different ways. Understand?"

He waits until Faith gestures that she has heard before he continues. "OK, so once upon a time, the Abbot of Sera Monastery, or rather the ex-Abbot of Sera Monastery, a holy man, an irreplaceable Buddhist master, sat meditating whilst overlooking a holy lake..."

"Who you become in pursuit of the goal will have more impact than the goal ever will..." ~ Paul Blackburn

Chapter 34

Faith talks animatedly with Randy; unfortunately, she is not making any sense. Faith can see his confusion, so she tries talking more slowly, but slow gibberish is just as hard to understand as fast gibberish. Faith repeats herself but repeated gibberish is, well, you get it.

"When the incarnation of the Dakini marked by the tear of the dragon is found by her mirror, the chains of the dragon will melt from the land of snows."

Randy nods and tries to keep a neutral face, figuring that if Faith keeps talking for long enough, he will eventually work out what the hell she is going on about.

"Don't you see? I am the Dakini with the tear of the dragon." Faith points to the birthmark that today is filled in with white make-up and is outlined in a red that matches the color of her lipstick. Faith was starting to like her birthmark, her birthright. "Tenzin," and she points to Tenzin who is still in a coma, "Tenzin is my mirror."

"Ummm." Still nothing, but Randy smiles encouragingly.

"Tenzin's eyes are the mirror image of mine. So when she finds my reincarnation the chains of the dragon will melt away, right?"

Fortunately, Faith is only half talking to Randy. The other person she is talking to is herself. "But I should be dead by now and I'm not and Tenzin is in a coma, not me."

Faith stares at Tenzin. She looks like she is in a deep sleep. Faith sends a silent request to her friend, 'Please wake up Tenzin, please.'

"So, I think… rather, I know… that I'm meant to be doing something… besides my meditation and practice... something that only I can do..."

Faith hobbles up and down the room. Randy tries to turn invisible, but it doesn't work. Faith continues, "Something really big, bold, and ballsy to start to melt those chains while my mirror is… asleep. Any ideas, Randy?"

Randy shakes his head 'No'; he had no idea. However, he feels he needs to chime in, "I'm sure I'll come up with something. Faith, tell me a bit more about those 'chains'…"

Tenzin's internal injuries have stabilized. Her condition is still serious, but she is no longer in the intensive care ward. Faith wastes no time in personalizing Tenzin's private suite. The hospital staff were not keen on the redecoration, but Faith bulldozed them. She knew the changes would help Tenzin's recovery and on this hospital turf, she gets her way.

Faith agreed to leave all the hospital-issued bed linen as they were, but she had brought Tenzin's altar and all of the wall hangings, thangkas, and statues of Buddha from her room in the apartment.

A small tea light was burning on the altar and there was a hint of sandalwood in the air. It had taken a while to find the spot and the clean burning candles that would not trigger the sprinkler system.

David stands next to Faith as they look down at Tenzin. She looks peaceful. Faith rearranges the covers.

"You haven't really had the chance to meet her yet… you'll like her."

David looks around. On the wall behind Tenzin's bed are two beautiful thangkas; one is of the Medicine Buddha and the other is White Tara, the Goddess of Universal Compassion.

Faith notices David noticing, "I bought the White Tara from the Dharma Center."

David says nothing for a while. He clears his throat, twice. Looking at Tenzin he says, "Faith, you may have to consider appointing another trustee for your Next Life Fund."

Faith pretends that she has not heard David. Finally, he comes over to Faith's side of the bed and squeezes her hand before he leaves.

Faith is sitting upright, meditating in front of an altar. The altar is in Tenzin's private hospital room. There is a knock at the door. It takes Faith a moment to come back. She remains sitting.

"Come in."

Rinpoche comes in and smiles. Faith moves to get up, but he waves for her to stay where she is.

"Ahhh, Faith, how is your practice?"

"Better Rinpoche, it is getting easier. Now that I have stopped fighting it... I am enjoying it."

Rinpoche nods and walks over to Tenzin. He takes her wrist, checking her pulse. He waves his hand over her closed eyes. There is no response, not that he expected any. Rinpoche pulls up a cushion next to Faith.

"I... I feel like when I'm meditating here that, well, that I connect with Tenzin, that she knows I am here."

Rinpoche nods, "You honor your friend by taking your practice deeper... As you may have already guessed, you have a strong connection to each other, one that goes back many lifetimes."

Not so long-ago Faith would have blown off such a comment as new-age do-gooder claptrap before moving as far away as possible from the person saying it. Now, she simply nods her head. She knew it was true.

"Rinpoche, what do you think? Will Tenzin come out of the coma?"

Rinpoche takes his glasses off and cleans the lenses carefully. He unwraps his prayer beads from his wrist before replying.

"That is a difficult question. Her injury is grave but there are many, many, prayers being said for Tenzin's recovery, and she is strong." They both look across to the bed.

"Faith."

"Yes?"

Rinpoche smiles, "We must have faith, Faith. There are no accidents. Your name is not an accident. Do you have faith?"

"Faith? Faith in what, Rinpoche?"

"Do you have faith?"

"I... I don't know, Rinpoche. Faith in what?"

Rinpoche stares at Faith until she breaks eye contact, "Ahh…"

"Rinpoche, if Tenzin doesn't get better does that mean that the prophecy will fail?"

Instead of answering Rinpoche says, "I have asked the Gyuto Monks to do a Karma Clearing Puja for Tenzin and for you, here. It is a powerful ceremony. Now, if you like, I will meditate with you."

Faith is honored to meditate with Rinpoche. Together they assume the meditation position and Faith goes deeper in her practice than she has ever experienced before.

Tenzin's hospital room is lit only by the single candle carefully placed on the altar. Faith is sitting in a chair next to Tenzin, holding her hand, and talking to her.

"Tenzin, you don't have to do this to get me to do practice. I am practicing, honest. I'm not mucking around anymore… I promise I'll be a better student, really, really, just come back… I miss you."

After a discreet knock, Nurse Mandy comes into the room to change Tenzin's drip. She can't believe that Faith is the same person who had thrown bedpans at walls only months earlier. Who would have thought? Not her. Not her friend Wendy either.

"There would be no chance to get to know death at all ... if it happened only once." ~ *Sogyal Rinpoche*

Chapter 35

Six saffron-robed Gyuto Monks sit on a raised platform on intricately woven Tibetan prayer rugs. Their chanting fills the room and beyond. David and a few members of the Dharma Center, including Patty, sit silently in chairs, eyes closed, thumbs touching their middle fingers, letting the amazing sound wash over and through them as they pray for Tenzin's recovery.

The Gyuto Monks are masters of deep harmonic overtone chanting. Each monk can chant in three octaves at once. Their training takes many years. The chanting is punctuated by the sound of Tibetan cymbals, horns, and bells. It is an auditory and visual feast.

Faith is sitting next to Tenzin's bed; her eyes are closed. Her head is up. She has entered a deep meditative state...

... Her head is shaved. She is sitting in a prayer room full of sister nuns in an ancient Tibetan monastery. They are all facing a treasured, 20-foot-high gold leaf-covered statue of Buddha. The smoke, smell, and fluttering light of hundreds of butter lamps fill the room.

Faith's voice joins the chanting of the Namo Ratna Mantra, the Great Compassion Mantra. At the appropriate times, she picks up her shang, her handbell, and rings it. The sound of a hundred voices and a hundred bells vibrate through the stone and every person. Faith has never felt more at peace. She turns and looks at the nun sitting next to her. It is Tenzin.

Tenzin leans forward and pins the robes of the nun in front of her to her cushion. Faith smiles and closes her eyes…

… Faith opens her eyes as the last echo of the Gyuto Monk's chanting fades to silence, a blissful silence that is not broken for several minutes. The audience bows appreciatively to the monks who step down from the platform. Wherever Tenzin was, she would have been aware of that ceremony.

Tenzin's room is dark except for flickering candlelight. Shadows chase each other across the ceiling. Faith sits cross-legged on a cushion with her back against the wall, eyes closed. Her head lolls to one side.

The quiet is shattered by the ringing of Faith's mobile phone. Faith jolts awake. Ineptly she tries to answer the call to stop the discordant sound. It is Randy. This had better be good.

"Randy! Randy… Slow down! Which channel?"

Faith picks up the remote and is relieved when the TV, high on the wall in front of Tenzin's bed turns on. She turns the volume up and flicks through until she finds the BBC1 channel.

A reporter finishes an interview before the program cuts to Nelson's 169-foot-high Column in Trafalgar Square, London. The camera zooms in on a figure standing on top of the Column. They unfurl a giant 50-foot-long banner. The banner is dominated by a smiling photo of the Dalai Lama. His hands are joined in the traditional 'Namaste' position. In red, above the Dalai Lama's head is the word "Reward.". The banner has a Wild West 'Wanted' poster feel to it. The bottom of the poster consists of the word, "Peace."

"Reward the Dalai Lama? Oh, I hope so," says Faith.

At the base of Nelson's Column fire engine sirens scream and police constables hold back a large crowd. The person who unfurled the banner steps to the edge. It looks as if they are about to jump. Faith gasps. They jump. Faith drops her phone.

There is a terrifying silence. The shocked crowd holds its breath as the body plummets toward the ground. With a fraction of a second left to save his life, a parachute erupts from a backpack and the BASE jumper lands safely. There is a necessary inhale before the crowd erupts cheering and whistling their appreciation. WOW! He could have died.

159

Faith picks up the phone, "Amazing! Perfect! I love it! Find out who did it... I want to meet them, pronto."

The image of the huge banner of the Dalai Lama fluttering gently in the wind stays with Faith. She turns to Tenzin and holds her hand, "Maybe the key can start to turn before I die." It wasn't talking to yourself if somebody else was in the room, was it?

There is a new framed photo of the Dalai Lama on the altar in Tenzin's room. It is one of His Holiness laughing and it is Faith's favorite. Rinpoche is meditating with Faith again.

He leans forward, picks up his Tibetan chimes, and rings them, ending their session. As the sound fades, Faith comes back. Rinpoche turns to face her. He picks up Faith's hand and taps on her wrist. He repeats this process on her other arm before he looks into her eyes.

"You are dying."

Faith surprises herself with her response. "We are all dying."

Yeshe Trichen Rinpoche smiles as he says, "Indeed."

Faith feels that her time is getting closer. Her symptoms were getting worse. She was finding it easier to meditate but harder to concentrate as if that made sense. Every day was getting harder. But she could not pass away yet, no way.

"I will not die without saying goodbye to Tenzin. She promised to be with me when I entered the Bardo and... I want... I believe... in her."

"Ah... then Achala, we must pray that Tenzin recovers swiftly."

They both look at their comatose friend. She looked like she was sleeping. Her body was on the bed but where was her mind?

Tenzin is meditating in the mouth of a cave. The picture quality was a little foggy, but she was sitting on a ledge that had a panoramic view over a verdant valley. Behind her, water trickles down the rock face and conveniently collects in a basin in the rock that is surrounded by red and yellow wildflowers.

In front of Tenzin is a sutra that she is chanting, page by page. To her right is her dorje and bell. She has found her cave in the snow; it is perfect, and she does not want to leave but...

The towering, rugged snowcapped mountains embrace the valley. The sun peaks from behind a cloud and as it touches the white snow it shines so brightly that Tenzin has to shade her eyes.

160

In the hospital room, Randy is preparing for a presentation. He shifts the data projector so that its bright light shines on the wall and not in Tenzin's face. Once he has the projector in position and focused, the lights are dimmed. He plays the complete video footage from the Nelson's Column "Reward the Dalai Lama" stunt. Faith had tuned in late and had missed the opening interview with Isabel Losada, the stunt organizer. The clip runs to its triumphant conclusion. Faith claps in appreciation.

Faith's health, as Rinpoche had noted, is deteriorating, rapidly. Would Dr. Kleinstein be happy that the disease was now progressing 'normally?'

The lights come back on. Isabel is sitting in the room along with David and Faith. Isabel is attractive and tall and she has a presence.

"So, Isabel, congratulations! I understand that you did all that... and got worldwide publicity with a budget of only 5,000 pounds?" Faith is impressed. She had once spent that on a hotel room for one night and she had, fortunately, managed to get no publicity for what she got up to.

Isabel nods, she is both jet-lagged and excited by this meeting. She had read about Faith McCormack who was something of a legend and Randy had filled her in on her change of heart and adoption of the Tibetan cause. Imagine what could be done with a decent budget? Isabel could.

"Well, we have no budget for what I want to do."

Isabel is confused by Faith's statement. "I don't understand. No budget? But ... but then why did you fly me here? It cost you almost as much to get me here as..."

Faith holds up her hand to forestall further protest and she laughs, though the laugh turns into an unhealthy hacking cough. Only after the coughing has subsided can Faith continue. "Sorry, what I mean is that we are effectively budget less... we have no monetary restrictions limiting what we can do, within reason."

Isabel peers at her through her jet lag, "I'm sorry, say again?"

"Well, you know, when I say budget less, I think we should try to keep the costs below $100 million or so, not including Randy or David's fees."

"$100 million? Keep the costs below $100 million? You have that kind of money for the Tibetan cause? You're serious?"

Faith smiles, "I assure you, Isabel, I am deadly serious."

Faith's emphasis on the word 'deadly' makes both David and Randy wince. They were both very concerned about Faith. She should be resting, conserving her strength, instead of doing this.

"This is highly confidential but there is a prophecy that has come out of Tibet, a crucial one, one that predicts the end of Chinese oppression in Tibet, a free Tibet if you will. Tenzin…" and she indicates the figure lying in the hospital bed, "brought this prophecy out of Tibet…"

She looks at her friend and remembers the first time she saw her when she still wore the scars of her attempted escape and subsequent deportation. It reminds Faith that she must thank the Senator who had written the letter that had ultimately saved Tenzin's life. A generous donation to his re-election campaign would be a nice way to say thank you for saving Tibet.

Everyone is waiting for Faith to continue. She is oblivious to the disconnect between what she thinks is a momentary pause and the minute it takes before she resumes talking.

"… and while I still draw breath and oddly, I admit, even afterward, I will do all I can to make this prophecy come true. You are not the only ones to have been moved and inspired by Tibetans." Faith smiles at Isabel. "It is almost annoying."

Faith looks up. "Randy?"

"Isabel, Faith's vision is inspired by your success. What she would like to do is expand your idea up to a national and international scale, including leveraging activism with paid advertising. But, we will need a lot of experienced people to pull it off on such a scale."

Isabel nods, "I'm pretty sure that the Students for a Free Tibet and the International Campaign for Tibet will be keen to help. There are quite a few other Tibet support organizations too."

Faith pipes up, "Great. Randy you and Isabel get cracking. David is project manager and legal counsel. Let's not break too many laws, Isabel." Faith pauses and grins, "But let's bend as many as we possibly can."

"Hmmm, let me see... $100 million. Excuse me while I pinch myself. Ouch! OK - I'm awake. Wow. OK - so how long do we have?"

"Ah, well, that… that… we don't have much time. Rinpoche is starting a three-day divination ritual to find the most auspicious launch date for us. I need to have a little rest now, Randy can you look after Isabel please?"

Randy offers Isabel his arm and they leave the room. Isabel keeps looking back toward Faith until the door finally closes behind them. David stays in the room. He also stares at Faith but with a bemused smile on his face. He shakes his head.

"What? What?" Faith is a little defensive. Whenever she has seen that look from David in the past she has been in trouble. David does not respond immediately. He gets up, picks up his briefcase, and walks over to Faith. He kisses her gently on the head.

"You seem so, kind of... well, almost happy… and your best friend, well..." He waves at Tenzin. "And to top it off, you're dying."

Faith pokes her tongue out at David, "I'm dying?"

Together Faith and David both say, "We're all dying" and they laugh, enjoying their joke. Faith points towards the image still projected on the wall.

"I'm looking forward to this."

"So Faith, do you still want to try and take it all with you?"

Faith is mesmerized by the image of Nelson's Column with the huge banner of the Dalai Lama hanging from it. It takes a while for Faith to realize that David was talking to her.

"Oh, that." She laughs. "We can leave the trust as it is, but I'd like to do a new will tomorrow. Right now, what I need to do is meditate, can you just help me...?"

David helps Faith move in front of the room's altar. He lowers her onto the cushion and notices an intricately inscribed Tibetan singing bowl. David takes the polished wooden mallet and rubs it around the rim of the bowl until the bowl begins to sing.

In the Dharma Center, a larger prayer bowl vibrates and the song hovers and ebbs to silence. Rinpoche is with monks and nuns who have just completed a three-day divination ritual.

The answer to questions regarding Faith's plan had been asked. Six identical dough balls were prepared. Different responses were written on fine pieces of paper and baked into them. The 'yes' ball had seemingly jumped out of the bowl.

Rinpoche removes the cover from a special bowl that had been sitting in front of a thangka of Paldon Lhamo, the principal protectress deity of Tibet. There are four identical dough balls in this bowl.

Rinpoche holds the bowl in his hands. Mantras are chanted as he gently moves it in a circular motion. The speed of the rolling balls increases until one eventually flies out.

Before he breaks apart the dough ball, Rinpoche licks his lips. After breaking the ball open, he removes the paper and reads the message. He whistles between his teeth.

Faith works on her laptop in the mini office she has set up in Tenzin's private hospital room. A formerly proficient touch typist, Faith's typing has degenerated to a 'hunt and peck' methodology with regular misses. It is frustrating.

Rinpoche knocks and enters the room. He looks exhausted and, for the first time, apprehensive.

He hands Faith the slip of paper from the dough ball. Faith looks at the paper and back at Rinpoche without changing her expression. Rinpoche admires her nerve.

"It's written in Tibetan."

"Ah, sorry, of course. The good news is that we have found a highly auspicious date. Success is almost guaranteed."

Faith stares at Rinpoche waiting for the other news.

"The date is only three weeks away."

Faith is surprised, after a pause she nods. She had done the impossible before for money, she would do it again for something a little more important.

"I will be giving teachings at the Dharma Center tonight. Can you make it?"

Faith looks over at Tenzin and then at Rinpoche. Rinpoche walks over to Tenzin. He checks her pulse on both of her wrists and then he smiles.

"Tenzin will be fine. I can feel her life force, her pulse, getting stronger. That is good news. Your dedication, the prayers, and pujas have all helped."

Before he leaves, Rinpoche goes to the altar, lights a candle, and chants. He knows they are going to need every prayer they can get.

"A small body of determined spirits fired by an unquenchable faith in their mission can alter the course of history." ~ Mahatma Gandhi

Chapter 36

Randy and Isabel hit the ground running. Both are no-nononsense doers, and they complement each other, not as in "Oh, you look great today," but as in Randy's weaknesses were Isabel's strengths and vice versa. No one could believe that they had known each other for less than 48 hours.

They reach out, rally, and enroll two of the oldest, largest, and most active Tibetan support organizations in the world; Students for a Free Tibet (SFT) and the International Campaign for Tibet (ICT).

The first meeting is being held at the Omni Hotel in Philadelphia. The location was approximately halfway between the two international headquarters of Washington D.C. and New York City respectively and it was poignant for another reason. The hotel was opposite Independence Park, a National Historical Park that includes the Liberty Bell and Independence Hall where the Declaration of Independence was signed.

The 13th Dalai Lama issued the Proclamation of Tibetan Independence in 1913 and whilst Tibet enjoyed 36 years of full independence it remained isolated behind its mountainous borders and its membership of the United Nations was not finalized. China violated international law when it invaded Tibet in 1950.

In 1950 the world was recovering from World War II and India from the nightmare of partition. Communist Russia had been decimated by the war and the butcher, Joseph Stalin, was in charge so it is sad, but not surprising, that the world community did nothing to help Tibet. Perhaps if Tibet had had vast oil reserves it would have been different?

Freedom is a word that has many meanings. Freedom for Tibet once unequivocally meant independence; a return to Tibet as it was before it was invaded by its large and densely populated neighbor; a return to a Tibet free from any Chinese involvement or control of religion or government or defense. Over the decades that position has been maintained by many Tibetans and is still maintained by the Students for a Free Tibet.

Every year since 1950 has been painful for Tibetans in Tibet and for the Tibetans who are refugees in other countries. Even though Tibetans have been refugees for decades they still have to report to police stations to maintain their refugee status.

In Tibet, Tibetans suffer religious persecution, the frenzied exploitation of rich forests and mineral deposits, the corralling of nomads, and the systematic dismantling of the Tibetan way of life. The forced migration of millions of Han Chinese into the ironically named Tibetan Autonomous Region has made Tibetans second-class citizens and a minority in their own country. Street signs are in Mandarin, and it is also the language of business. China has engaged in cultural genocide but despite this, despite all this, Tibetans have struggled non-violently to regain their freedom.

The Chinese Government has been intractable. Agreements to enter dialogue ignored both in physical attendance and in spirit if they do show up. Meanwhile, the violent military crackdowns within Tibet of offenses as shocking as possessing a photo of the Dalai Lama are punished harshly, violently, lethally.

In the face of all this, despite broken promise after broken promise, His Holiness the Dalai Lama and the Tibetan Government in Exile have made huge compromises. They are willing to accept freedom to mean actual autonomy for Tibet within China; think Scotland within the United Kingdom.

The International Campaign for Tibet supports the middle-path approach. Unfortunately, this vast compromise is met with disdain from China instead of being met with respect and awe. His Holiness is constantly vilified by China. Chinese leaders use all their vast economic and military might to intimidate and threaten leaders of countries if they so much as agree to meet with His Holiness who, in addition to being a world-renowned religious leader, Congressional Gold Medal recipient, Nobel Peace Laureate and one of only a few authors to ever have multiple books on the New York Times Best Seller list at the same time.

Everyone in the room is all too aware of the significance of the location for this meeting and the deteriorating conditions within Tibet. They are also all committed to making a difference.

Faith is wheelchair bound and it both grates on her and makes life easier too. When she is moving from one place to another, she is so grateful for her wheels and for the blanket on her lap. When she is sitting and would rather be prowling back and forth dominating and driving a meeting, like now, it annoys her, but not nearly as much as it would have a short time ago.

Normally it would take a minimum of four to six months to plan, secure manpower and support materials, arrange for publicity, and execute an outside activist event like Nelson's Column. To run a campaign with upwards of 30 individual events, incorporating paid advertising could take over a year of planning or more.

Whilst both SFT and the ICT are international organizations they have slightly different focuses and many members support both. SFT has a younger demographic, is organized into hundreds of chapters, mostly at schools and Universities, and is more direct grassroots education and activism focused. Students for a Free Tibet advocate for Tibet's complete independence.

The International Campaign for Tibet supports the middle path approach and is particularly effective in lobbying politicians and high-profile personalities to support the Tibetan cause and inspire lasting policy changes. With over 100,000 supporters worldwide it has an older demographic than SFT.

Despite the lack of notice, directors from both organizations are sitting around a table with David, Isabel, and Randy. There is an undeniable air of excitement; however, the air pressure that had built up over the past hour had been punctured somewhat when the launch date had been disclosed.

Paul from the SFT tries to summarize their feelings, "Look, you know, this sounds great, amazingly ambitious… but…" Of course, there was an incoming 'but,' the longer the interlude before the 'but,' the bigger the 'but' would be, "There is just not enough time. It would take us over a week just to email our chapters to gauge interest, and we need an extra week to mail out info. We either cancel most of the stunts or we do it later, several months later, when we can be prepared and make the most of it."

The other representatives reluctantly, but firmly, nod their heads in agreement. A few mutter, "Sorry."

Faith has been listening up till now, letting Randy and Isabel outline the approach, the elements, the targets, and the resources that will be made available and what would be required to pull it off. She stands up and leans forward, using the table to support her. Even the least observant could see the supreme effort it takes.

"Firstly, I want to acknowledge every one of you." Faith looks every person in the eye as she is speaking. "And thank you for your commitment, your dedication to the Tibetan people, to a peaceful solution. I know it has not been easy… I know that what we are proposing sounds unreasonable, a bit mad even." There is general agreement. Faith's voice becomes louder and deeper, "Isn't it time we gave unreasonable and a bit mad a try?"

Faith leaves her question hanging before she continues. "When was the last time you had a virtually unlimited budget for an international campaign? For any campaign"

"Only in my dreams," sighs Meagan, fundraising manager for the ICT.

"Exactly! This is a dream come true. I have the will and the money to back this but even more importantly; this proposal has the support of Yeshe Trichen Rinpoche and the most senior masters of each of the four schools of Tibetan Buddhism. They urge you to support this because it is part of a larger prophecy, a prophecy that will result in a free Tibet. Know this, the go date is not negotiable, it is not a date that we would have chosen, it is a date that has chosen us."

Faith has a well-deserved reputation for being intimidating. In the past, she fueled her passion with the primal adrenalin rush of regular financial battles. She hated and had also become addicted to, her fuel source. Faith's desire to prove herself; to escape poverty and become the best of the best, drove her back to the market front lines long after she knew that it was time for her to leave, that it was unhealthy for her to stay.

Bernhard had understood Faith. He had exploited her ruthlessly and he had used Chuck to keep Faith's fight reflex constantly engaged. Via Chuck, Bernhard had provided Faith with a thick, in more ways than one, vein of adrenalin that when tapped, was sweeter and more righteous than the adrenalin high of beating the market.

For the first time in her life, her heart was fueling her passion. It was not the adrenalin of the fight egging her on, it was something new, a belief in something bigger than herself. Faith was no longer just formidable; she was now a force to be reckoned with.

"Together we can and will deal with every obstacle and every bottleneck that we face. I know it will cost more money to get things done quickly. I am totally fine with that. So, who is with us?"

People had been holding their breath without realizing it; once there was sufficient oxygen there were shouts of, "Hell yeah," "Absolutely," and "Yes!" Except for David, no one else in the room had ever seen Faith in full flight and even for David, this was something new.

Faith's audience now believed everything they had heard and read about her, except for some of the more unsavory bits. Crucially, they believed that when Faith set her sights on something, it happened, even if everyone said it was impossible, it would still happen.

"Randy... whiteboard. Let's list everything we need from a list of targets to personnel, all the way down to banners and stencils. We need short, sharp, focused meetings, and quick responsive lines of communication. We have the advantage in that we know what needs to be done."

"We are replicating on a massive scale a combination of Isabel's Nelson's Column stunt, the energy and funk of SFT's Free Tenzin Delek Rinpoche campaign, and the ongoing ICT success in lobbying key politicians. Let's identify logjams and potential blockages... tonight. Rooms are available for anyone who doesn't want to drive back. But before we get into it... Let's share a meal."

Randy leaves the room and moments later a delicious buffet dinner is set up on a long table. Whilst the food is being served, the electronic whiteboard is prepared with columns ranging from logistics to security to legal to media.

Faith sits back down in her wheelchair. She felt energized by what she was doing but just standing up for long was becoming difficult.

Sharing good food is a time-honored way of connecting. Some of the people in the different organizations had met before and were delighted to catch up with old friends; others were meeting new friends for the first time. After everyone is fed and watered the serious business of task-mapping responsibilities begins.

Given the sensitive nature of Homeland Security towards iconic landmarks, each target location was to be given a Tibetan code name. The Goddess Tara had yellow, orange, pink, black, and grey aspects. Vertical "Reward" banners were shawls, horizontal banners were cloaks, graffiti stencils were black mandalas and so it went on. In the so-called Land of the Free, government officials had become less and less tolerant of the people asking for what they wanted by peacefully demonstrating.

As the process mapping continues it becomes clear that, due to the volunteer base for each organization, it was going to be difficult to get the 100% focus and follow-up required to pull this off at such short notice. Both organizations had effective systems with hundreds of active supporters between them, but only a few paid positions and everyone was already swamped with their current workloads.

As the discussion on the availability of the man and woman power required spirals downwards Faith steps in with a well-aimed question, "How many people are dedicated to fundraising?"

Both fundraising managers respond at the same time, "A lot, unfortunately."

Faith looks at David; she was starting to flag. It had been quite a full lifetime.

"OK. David, please arrange a substantial donation to both organizations so they can pull everyone off fundraising duties without losing any revenue. Plus, enough to pay volunteers to go full-time for six weeks."

David makes a note in his phone. It would be done and done swiftly. "We need people dedicated to this campaign. The questions I want to hear now are 'How can we make this bigger? Global?' Flash mobs, lots of videos distributed via social media. You have the infrastructure already in place for us to do this. Clear?"

There is a babble of excitement. Faith's no-nonsense approach is infectious.

The whiteboard is full, the breakout groups have co-operated on task allocations and responsibilities and the momentum is wavering. Everyone has been going hard for a long while and it is time to call it a night. Those who stay will finish tidying things up in the morning.

Randy, poised with a black texta over the Media column asks, "One last question. Faith, you are going to be the spokesperson for the media? Aren't you?"

"No, Tenzin will be."

Randy and David both stop what they are doing; they look at each other uneasily. Neither of them wants to say anything, nonetheless, something needs to be said.

"But Faith… Faith, she is still..."

"Tenzin will be! Remember to include her in your prayers." And that was that. Faith was taking being unreasonable and making it the norm and no one was going to argue with her.

"Beginning today, treat everyone you meet as if they were going to be dead by midnight. Extend them all the care, kindness, and understanding you can muster. Your life will never be the same again." ~ Og Mandino

Chapter 37

After the meetings, they fly back to Chicago just in time to attend Rinpoche's standing-room-only talk. Rinpoche has a beautiful understanding of Dharma; he makes it accessible and easy to understand. The entire room spends five minutes praying for Tenzin.

After the talk, people queue to receive a blessing from Rinpoche. The line is long and a Chinese couple, Chen and Yun Il wait patiently. They have traveled hundreds of miles and, finally, it is their turn.

"Rinpoche, we have come to ask you for a... a fertility blessing, please." They offer Rinpoche khatas and they lean forward. Rinpoche says a special prayer in Tibetan for them and puts their khatas back around their necks.

Chen and Yun Il bow and walk away. Chen looks across at a woman sitting in a wheelchair. She appears to be dozing, but Chen feels that something is not right, so he walks over to check on her. He asks if she is OK but there is no reply. He tries to wake her, gently at first but there is no response.

Chen checks the woman's pulse; he is relieved to detect it but it is faint and fluttering. His manner becomes urgent, and he shouts.

"Rinpoche! Someone, please call an ambulance!"

While Faith's body remains in the wheelchair she is no longer there. As Faith looks down at her body, she is surprised. She is also relieved that she no longer feels any pain. Faith watches as Rinpoche races over to her. He immediately takes hold of her hands and begins chanting in Tibetan. Faith can hear him clearly; her body can hear him and so can her spirit. She can feel the prayers pulling on her.

Chen rushes into the room with the paramedics. Dr. Chen is wearing a stethoscope.

Faith can see a bright light. It is warm and alluring and she is so tired, so exhausted. She wants to go towards the light, but she can hear Rinpoche's prayers calling her. The attraction of the light is stronger than the pull of the prayers. She takes one final backward glance at her body but behind her wheelchair, she notices a photo of Tenzin on a prayer altar. Tenzin, dear Tenzin. The light? Tenzin? Tenzin. She can't abandon Tenzin. Can she? It would be so easy to let go but instead, she follows the sound of the prayers. Faith uses them to guide her back into her deteriorating body.

Tenzin's private suite is now a double room. Faith is breathing with the help of oxygen. She has a drip in her arm. She has only just been transferred from intensive care, stable, but weak. A full-time nurse is in attendance. Faith's eyes flicker open momentarily before she falls back to sleep. She is too weak to even scratch the incessant itch on her hand.

Back at the Dharma Center, the altar set up for Tenzin also has a photo of Faith on it, in addition to the photos of Rinpoche, Rinpoche's teachers, and the Dalai Lama. The altar is in the meditation room. Candles burn brightly.

The Center had sent out an email for Tenzin and Faith to be remembered in prayers. Ten people are in the room meditating and praying.

The photo of Tenzin has captured her when she was laughing. It is a great photo.

Tenzin is still in a coma and Faith is finally sleeping peacefully. The TV in the room had been left on, but the programming has finished, and the screen has gone all snowy...

It is snowy for Tenzin too. She is sitting in a lotus position on the ledge outside of her cave, surrounded by mountains and overlooking the green valley. Thunder rumbles and snow falls, muffling the thunder and blanketing her ledge. Tenzin and the area around her remain snow-free even though the flakes that flutter down are so thick and close together that they white out Tenzin's vision...

...For Tenzin, the white of the Himalayan snow has turned to a sea of white khata scarfs being thrown jubilantly in the air by a crowd that lines the road that winds through Lhasa, Tibet, and leads to the Potala Palace, the home of the Dalai Lama.

Words struggle to capture the scene. 'Joyous' is a useful word, a good word but it falls short. Imagine feeling euphoric. Now imagine putting all that in a glass bottle with just enough bliss to let it ferment. Put a tight lid on it and then bury the bottle under layer upon layer of suffering and persecution for 60 years or more.

Finally, when hope is all but dead and euphoria a forgotten emotion, dig up that bottle and stand back when you pop the cork. As the decompressed concoction of euphoria and joy gushes out into enthusiastic ecstasy, spray it everywhere. The crowd has been doused in just such a potent mix which is highly contagious.

The cloud of white scarfs obscure the road. The thunder gets louder and gradually it becomes discernible as the sound of hundreds of Tibetan trumpets being blown by a procession of saffron-robed monks and nuns. The color of their robes is in stark contrast to the white of the scarfs.

Following hundreds of monks and nuns is a platform that is supported by poles carried on the proud shoulders of large bald monks. On the platform sits His Holiness the 14th Dalai Lama. He is riding the waves of elation and he is so happy he seems to glow. Tears stream unashamedly down his cheeks. To be back in his beloved Tibet, to see and feel the people celebrating...

As the procession reaches the steps of the Potala Palace, the crowd changes from general public to dignitaries. The notables include high-ranking Chinese officials as well as Presidents, Prime Ministers, and celebrities from around the world. Certain Chinese officials refused to be intoxicated by the exultation whilst others were already in rapture. These latter men and women had risked their reputations and their lives to bring this about and, behold, it was good, very good.

China had underestimated the amount of global goodwill that granting Tibet freedom had generated. One act at the right time can have profoundly positive ramifications for the future of humankind. The leaders responsible would be remembered forever for their courage whilst those that had abused their power were already forgotten.

It was being hailed as one of the great humanitarian wonders of the world, up there with the demolition of the Berlin Wall, the freeing of Nelson Mandela, the end of Apartheid, the Ghandi-inspired freeing of India, the apology by the Australian Government to Aboriginals and peace in Northern Ireland.

Everywhere it was welcomed as a sign of strength, confidence, and leadership by China. Peaceful means could produce results. Within China, this was also an important message as frustration with draconian, authoritarian leaders and corruption was all too quickly turning violent in many provinces. By allowing peaceful protests, corrupt officials were quickly identified and prosecuted which improved the Chinese economy and helped spread the prosperity instead of concentrating it in the hands of a few.

It was to result in a measurable increase in Chinese GDP as the annual skim by corrupt officials was reduced and global customers re-evaluated their feelings towards Chinese-made products. China's years of international bullying, running huge trade surpluses, bad environmental management, and an undeniably poor human rights record had been brewing discord across the world.

After so many years of violence around the world, the "Reward Peace" campaign had struck a chord that had resonated around the planet.

The global media are concentrated in a tight pack, and they have been given an excellent view of the Potala Palace. The cameras zoom in on young and wrinkled Tibetan men and women who are in bliss at seeing the Dalai Lama. There were also curious Han Chinese spectators, and they were contracting the contagion of the crowd.

Camera flashes sparkle from all sides. A film crew zooms in on a bystander. He is wearing a badge on his chest that is shaped like a key; as the camera pans over more of the crowd the same key can be seen over and over.

In a place of high distinction on the official podium, amongst senior monks and nuns, stands a very, very happy and older Tenzin. Next to her is an attractive Chinese child with a dragon tear birthmark under one eye. She is holding the hand of an older, doting, powerful media magnate. In visions, you can just tell these things. The wrinkles on this man's face crease readily into a smile. Everything fades to white.

175

Moments later, in the private hospital suite, a single tear sneaks down Tenzin's cheek and plops onto the pillow under her head. Her eyes flutter open. She can see the TV screen, but she has seen so much more. She has seen the prophecy fulfilled. She smiles and drifts into a contented sleep.

"You have to discover that the qualities of Buddhahood have always been inherently present within yourself." ~ Dilgo Khyentse Rinpoche

Chapter 38

Faith gradually wakes up to her hair being gently brushed. The first thing she does when she opens her eyes is to look over at Tenzin's bed. It is empty. Oh, no! She experiences a moment of panic before she realizes that it is Tenzin grooming her.

Faith looks up at her friend and is overwhelmed with joy. "I knew you'd come back," smiles Faith. Tenzin looks down at Faith and returns the smile.

"I made you a promise."

Faith's smile turns into a wicked grin.

"Oh, you are going to be so cranky when you find out what I've volunteered you for."

David has already visited and left along with other well-wishers. Randy is talking with Tenzin who is resting in her bed. A physiotherapist is massaging Tenzin's legs. The muscles had partially atrophied while she was in the coma, but she has had excellent care. A young Doctor is looking at Faith's chart.

"Tenzin, are you sure you are going to be well enough to be spokes nun?"

The Doctor signals to Randy: no way. Somehow Faith manages to give him a little kick which surprises everyone, especially the Doctor. Compassion is a wonderful thing and sometimes a little kick can feel good too. Tenzin looks at Faith and then Randy, ignoring the man in the white coat.

"Of course."

The command room for operation 'Turn the Key' is located in a large office block in Philadelphia. It was selected for its bandwidth and underground car park. Importantly, it is also close to a coffee house that makes a great cappuccino and a variety of quality takeaway restaurants that do not.

Access is via a card swipe system. They have been careful with security and the operation involves a large number of people from across the country. They were planning peaceful activism, not terrorism, but activists had been shut down for doing a lot less than what they were planning.

If Homeland Security picked up on 'chatter' they all prayed that the long history of non-violence of both organizations and the Tibetan cause would forestall any preemptive raids by authorities.

Maps and photos are pinned up across every wall. Each map is numbered, and contact details for each site are written neatly on the maps along with the code name. Tenzin is meeting the team for the first time. Randy and Isabel are with her. There are bags under everyone's eyes. No one has had much sleep. Everyone is excited to see Tenzin. She is feeling much better but tired easily.

They go over the logistics of the plan from start to finish. There had been challenges and delays on a daily, almost hourly basis. Each potential obstacle had been overcome. What this team had achieved in two and a half weeks went way beyond unreasonable, it was sensational. Fortunately, the timing had been good, and the grassroots of both Tibet support organizations had embraced the concept and were running hard with it.

Tenzin finishes speaking with the group, "... as you all know, peaceful. Absolutely no damage to property and nothing left behind when we have finished."

The group nods in agreement. One of the younger people present quips, "And nobody getting shot."

Tenzin laughs, "Thank you, definitely no body piercing with bullets, they are very unhygienic."

Faith discharged herself from the hospital and returned to her home as soon as she could. Funny, she never used to call it a home. Faith always referred to it as her penthouse, sometimes as her apartment or crash pad.

She knew she was dying. Yes, everyone was dying, and she would beat almost 'everyone' to the grave. There was no way she was going to die in that hospital.

The penthouse has been transformed for Faith's return. Tenzin had softened the hard edges, and it looked and felt better. The large TV screens in each room were gone and more plants had been brought in. Fluffy was delighted with the changes and she was as excited as a cat can be to see Faith.

Faith's bed had been replaced by an upmarket hospital bed. It could be wheeled from the bedroom to the lounge room or the kitchen. Not that Faith was likely to ever spend time in the kitchen. She had never spent any time there when she was well, so the chances of her going in now were unlikely.

Faith appreciates the view over Lake Michigan; it is an amazing lake. It is the only Great Lake that lies entirely within the United States and the largest freshwater sand dunes in the world are found on its shore. Today, sheets of rain were sweeping across the surface of the lake, whipping the white horses. The midday sun managed to momentarily peek through and shine a spotlight on the bright foam of the horses' manes.

Tenzin has been racking up frequent flyer points. Well, she would have if chartered flights gave frequent flyer credits. She has just flown from Philadelphia to New York via Chicago, which is about as indirect a route as it was possible to take.

Tenzin stands next to Faith's bed. Her bag, rarely unpacked, is at her feet. She is holding Faith's hand.

Rinpoche and David are standing on the other side of the bed. The rain drives against the windows. Faith tugs on David's sleeve. David opens a photo album and walks over to Tenzin. There is a photo of an unmarked, unkempt grave.

He flips to the next page. It is a photo of the same site, but the area has been cleaned up. There are flowers and a small Buddha in front of a new gravestone which is simply etched with "J. McCormack" and underneath the name, "He gave us life." "F. & T. McCormack."

Tenzin looks at this and nods to Faith, moved by her thoughtfulness. "I should stay here with you; you are so close. I promised. Randy can do the PR..."

Faith is having none of this. "Go. Go. Remember ..." Faith mumbles something but to Tenzin it is incoherent.

"Remember?"

Rinpoche coughs, he has heard. "I think she said remember... tits and ass?"

Faith gives a thumbs up.

*"If you can solve your problem, then what is the
need of worrying? If you cannot solve it, then what
is the use of worrying? ~ Shantideva*

Chapter 39

Tenzin is sitting with Randy on the chartered plane enroute to New York. A weather update appears on the satellite TV. They unmute it and lean forward expectantly.

A map of the US flashes up. Across the 48 states, the 24-hour forecast is shocking, unless you were a duck. But, given the cold fronts piling up, even the ducks would not be thrilled. Non-migratory birds would soon be talking with immigration. The forecast for New York was for thunderstorms and high winds.

They both grimace and then Tenzin slaps Randy on the thigh.

"Look at the bright side. With THAT forecast, if any red or red, white, and blue agency has heard about what we are planning and wants to stop us, they would never expect us to go ahead, would they? Huh?" She was so right but didn't know it.

"You're clutching at straws, Tenzin, but I like it. You know this whole auspicious date thing. Did you ever ask Rinpoche what he meant by success almost guaranteed? How much of an 'almost' are we dealing with?"

Tenzin looks back out the window. Lightning flashes across the sky.

They are lucky. A brief lull in the weather opens up just as they are about to be diverted and their aircraft scuttles in and lands.

Other flights are not so lucky. They are met as soon as they touch down and taken to the New York operations room.

The room resembles a military HQ. The New York organizers are both on the phones and they do not look happy. Whilst the room had a military crispness to it, everyone on the ground was a volunteer. After hanging up, Simon, a veteran activist comes over to Randy and Tenzin.

"Look, we are really sorry but we're going to have to abort. This weather is causing delays, we're running out of time and it's not safe out there. The shawls and cloaks are 60 feet long. Those become sails in high winds. Randy, we are just going to have to move to the backup date."

Tenzin looks up sharply at Randy who has the grace to look embarrassed and the wisdom to look away.

"No! No! Simon, there is no backup date. There has never been a backup date." Tenzin can feel herself breaking into a sweat.

She pulls herself together and breathes deeply, "Please, please. It must be tonight. Just ask everyone to wait a little longer. We do whatever we can safely do tonight... and continue to pray for a miracle."

Tenzin's prayer beads are moving rapidly through her fingers, any faster and she would get bead burn.

Orange witches' hats surround a large outside broadcast van parked on the edge of Times Square. The sides of the van have prominent, flashing "Filming in progress" neon signs on them. Tenzin and Randy are drenched as they race up to the back of the van. They knock as the rain starts to slacken.

They are immediately let in. There are 10 monitors in the van and three technicians. Tenzin is introduced to Dan who is in charge. One of the screens shows a live meteorological satellite view of the US with a zoomed-in window on New York state.

The cold fronts had moved through much faster than forecast leaving better weather behind them. Conditions would be cold and slippery because of all the precipitation but the strong winds were gone, and the rain reduced to isolated showers. Someone was looking after them, probably a deity or a couple of deities working together. Tenzin remembers to give thanks, but it doesn't stop her anxiety.

As darkness falls rain doesn't and Times Square comes to life. In the van, the technicians are in contact with ground teams equipped with cameras testing their wireless upload systems. It was going to be a very long night and day. The campaign was going to start when America woke up, they would find "Reward Peace", and "Reward the Dalai Lama" banners draped on, or hung from, many landmarks.

The outside broadcast van would ensure that all news outlets and TV stations would have high-definition feeds available for them to use. Teams in a hundred cities were using plastic stencils to create multi-colored plaster of Paris chalk "Reward" messages on sidewalks and on the sides of as many buildings as they could tag. Flash mobs would collect, perform, engage, and disappear only to repeat the colorful performance in a different high-traffic place. The best clips would be edited and put out via YouTube and social media sites.

One of the technicians taps Randy on the shoulder and leads him to the over-clocked laptop computer he has set up. The technician sits, clicks, hacks, and points. A number of the large signs in Times Square start to flash with "Reward the Dalai Lama", and "Reward Peace" followed by photos from Tibet.

On every lamp post around Times Square, a "Reward" poster has been taped and on hoardings, a chalk outline of the Dalai Lama's face has appeared with the words "Reward Peace" written underneath it.

As dawn breaks across the country, the full scale and success of the operation is gradually revealed. It is an otherwise slow news day with no plane crashes or crazed gunmen competing for headlines. Every morning show from every news channel runs with the story, even FOX. The footage is vibrant, colorful, positive, and free. After all the bad news the public is given a taste of something different.

Randy sits with headphones on. He has three phones in front of him and they have been ringing hot. He and Tenzin watch as images are uploaded from various locations.

The Empire State Building has a 'shawl' draped down it, the Liberty Arch is sporting a 'scarf' as a dapper accessory, Mount Rushmore, the Lincoln Memorial, and the feeds just keep coming in from a bridge here and a skyscraper there.

In Washington D.C. an armada of hot air balloons covered with light nylon "Reward Peace" and "Reward the Dalai Lama" coats move slowly and impressively across the Washington skyline.

Tenzin is ready for her first live interview. Behind her, the large five-story neon sign that dominates Times Square is flashing with paid advertising of the "Reward" campaign. The cameras were rolling.

"This is Cindy Mair reporting live from Times Square. We have an amazing spectacle unfolding across the country. I'm here with the spokes-nun, Tenzin Choedon..."

Meanwhile, in the Oval Office, the President of the United States is meeting with the Chinese President for vital informal talks. The visit is not official and has not been publicized. An Aide responds to a discreet knock on the door. To be interrupted it had to be important. After waiting for his opportunity, the Aide walks over to POTUS and whispers in his ear.

The President sighs, shakes his head, and whistles. He motions to the Aide. The Aide grabs a remote control. A section of the wall slides back to reveal four TV screens. POTUS turns to his guest.

"Mr. President, I am sorry for this interruption, but you may as well see this while you are here. It's all over the networks like a rash, regarding Tibet... um... the Tibetan Autonomous Region and rest assured, there is no way that they knew you were here... we are so sorry about this."

The sound is muted but they watch a smiling Tibetan Buddhist nun confidently speaking while over her left shoulder on the screens, behind a series of images flash across, one after the other: At the UN Building smaller "Reward" banners flutter under the flag of each of the UN countries. The Gateway Arch has a smiling photo of the Dalai Lama. There is a shot of fluttering Tibetan prayer flags hanging off the Statue of Liberty's torch. Banners are draped around her pedestal, careful not to obscure the chains that symbolize Liberty breaking free from bondage. The camera follows a flotilla of slow-moving hot air balloons floating majestically past the Washington Monument. Dozens of chalk outlines of the Dalai Lama on sidewalks across the nation are shown.

As the Chinese President watches, his face tightens but it is more surprise than anger. He straightens his tie pin. "Officially, of course, I am not here so I will say nothing, but I imagine that our ambassador will be... upset." He pauses, "But just between us, as with many nations, things were done a long time ago that we would not do today. Everything changes and we are changing too." The Chinese President gets to his feet and begins pacing.

He continues, "With the right kind of… encouragement, there is a possibility that we may be able to implement the cultural shifts necessary for true Tibetan autonomy, but we have to thwart hardliners within the party that still think the year is 1959."

Three of the TV screens in the Oval Office change back to Times Square and the warm, confident self-assured spokesperson, Tenzin. POTUS unmutes the main screen and the voice of the nun fills the room.

"… China is changing too. It will be good for China and good for Tibet for true autonomy to be granted and it will send an important… actually, a vital message to the world that peaceful struggles can be successful. It will be an amazing act of strength and world leadership when China returns the governance of Tibet within China back to Tibetans. Only a country as strong and confident as China could do this."

The advertising screen behind Tenzin displays a live feed of a parachutist with a vast banner beneath him. The banner waves as if it is alive. It reads "Remember Faith, Reward Peace." There is a huge smiling photo of His Holiness the Dalai Lama underneath the words. This banner was a special one-off dedicated to Faith. The Statue of Liberty is in the foreground with the banner fluttering some distance behind it.

Suddenly all the TV screens run the same TV commercial, as they do.

The 30-second commercial is a fast montage sequence of shots with a funky soundtrack. It has the theme "It is time, over 60 years of peaceful struggle is long enough… Reward the Dalai Lama, Reward the people of Tibet, Reward Peace."

Two of the signs in Times Square still display "Reward" but all the others have gone back to normal programming. A sweating Randy comes down the stairs of the OB van and picks Tenzin up in a bear hug. He twirls her jubilantly around.

David pulls up in a limo. He can't stop smiling and he bows his head to Tenzin who is overcome with emotion. She waves him in for the hug and he joins them. David returns to the car to retrieve a bottle of champagne which he pops. Unbelievably, and unreasonably, they had done it!

Tenzin proposes a toast "To Faith, the key to freeing Tibet."

They clink glasses and toast Faith.

David looks around at the van, the posters, the chalking and he laughs, "She's started to melt the chains already, hasn't she?"

Tenzin nods happily. The waiting limo is parked as far over as possible and the traffic is light but a motorist who had driven behind it would prefer to sit there and honk his horn rather than drive around. Ah, New York. The driver doesn't know it, but he is there to remind Tenzin that she cannot tarry.

"So, Tenzin, the hard part is about to start huh? It'll be like looking for a needle that can change haystacks."

"Finding Faith?... You know David, I have a strong feeling that..."

"That what?"

"That I'll find her. It's more than a strong feeling. I know I will find her, or she will find me. It may take a little while but what is so exciting is she has so many possible ways to fulfill the prophecy."

"She might be born in China, and she could marry a top party official or become a top party official and free Tibet that way or she might be born here and marry a global media mogul and melt his heart, providing he has one or, knowing Faith, she could become a media mogul herself. I can't wait to see what she does. I'm not worried, not anymore." Happy tears run down her cheeks.

Tenzin gives David a hug and then Randy.

The irritated but karmically perfect car driver rides his car horn. Tenzin has to go, she smiles.

"Congratulate everyone for me. They... you... are all awesome! Have a fantastic victory party. The jet's ready?"

David nods and holds the door of the limo open for Tenzin.

"Like nomads moving camp every season, we change our native land with every rebirth." ~ *Dilgo Khyentse Rinpoche*

Chapter 40

Tenzin bursts through the door and rushes to Faith. Faith is holding onto life, just. Rinpoche has already started the ritual. He is sitting on a cushion with his dorje and bell, reading from a sutra. He looks up and winks at Tenzin when she comes in, but his chanting does not stop.

Faith smiles when Tenzin takes her hand, she knows that Tenzin is there with her. Tenzin starts to cry, this time for herself. She will miss Faith. Faith tries to speak. Tenzin leans close. With great effort, Faith manages to whisper.

"My undies, not yours... thank you, thank you, thank you."

Faith can't laugh at her own joke, but she tries to grin. She looks peaceful, even happy as her spirit finally slips gently away from her body.

A magnificent vibrant double rainbow stretches across Lake Michigan. Tenzin looks out the window at it. More tears run down her cheeks. It is beautiful. Faith was a Dakini after all.

Slowly, gently, Tenzin lets go of Faith's hand and places it next to her body on the bed. She stares down for a moment longer and brushes a strand of hair away from Faith's blue eye.

Tenzin takes a deep breath and then breathes in even more deeply; she holds it and then releases it explosively. Rinpoche continues his chanting.

Tenzin goes to the little altar in the room and bows, she lights a candle below a photo of Faith and adds an incense stick to the incense that is already burning.

She retrieves her dorje, bell, and a sutra that is wrapped in a purple silk cloth from her bag. Tenzin moves a cushion next to Rinpoche and sets up her little reading table. She carefully unwraps the teaching and places it in front of her. She starts to chant along with her teacher.

Epilogue

Every major newspaper dedicated its front page to the activities of the "Reward the Dalai Lama", "Reward Peace" campaign which was a phenomenal public relations coup. The papers also carried articles and editorials supporting Tibet.

The influential Chicago Tribune broadsheet was an exception. It dedicated its home page to the sudden scandalous collapse of Napoleon Brothers. "Rogue Trader Razes Napoleon Brothers." The accompanying photo was a shot of a handcuffed Chuck Jones being marched toward a row of police cars. No white knight was willing to step in and save the oldest trading company in Chicago.

The activism continued and gathered momentum. Chalking of the "Reward" outline on buildings and billboards became a tagging competition and spread like a virus across the country, and the internet. People who had never heard about Tibet took notice and joined the clamor for fairness, for autonomy for Tibet.

The "Reward the Dalai Lama" message jumped oceans and into minds everywhere. In Australia, via the Australian Tibetan Council, a visiting Chinese dignitary was greeted by banners on both the Sydney Opera House and the Sydney Harbour Bridge.

Other landmarks around the world were tagged without damaging any of them. The statue of Jesus overlooking Rio de Janeiro asked the world to "Reward Peace." Red Square, the UK Houses of Parliament, the Eiffel Tower, and even the Great Wall of China temporarily asked the same thing.

After a change in Chinese leadership, progressive talks began in earnest with the Tibetan Government in Exile.

THE END

This book
has been inspired
by
His Holiness
the 14th Dalai Lama
and
the people of
Tibet.

Never Give Up

Never give up
No matter what is going on
Never give up.
Develop the heart.
Too much energy in your country is spent
developing the mind instead of the heart.
Develop the heart.
Be compassionate
Not just to your friends but to everyone,
Be compassionate.
Work for peace in your heart and in the
world.
Work for peace, and I say again
Never give up.
No matter what is happening
No matter what is going on around you,
Never give up.

~ H.H. the 14th Dalai Lama

Author's Note
There were many times when I wanted to give up on this
project. 'Never Give Up' helped keep me going and these
words continue to inspire me.

Acknowledgment

In June 2000, I was lucky enough to attend a talk by the Venerable Tenzin Palmo. After the talk finished, I outlined an idea that I had for a film. I nervously asked her if she thought the Tibetans would be OK with it? I will never forget how she laughed and said, "Go for it." I am so grateful for that encouragement.

I wrote *Taking it With You* as a script originally, because, naively, I had no inkling just how difficult it is to get a movie made. The delays and disappointments gave me time to make the story stronger.

The screenplay went through many drafts. My thanks to; James Harvey, Deb Cox, John Ackerly, Elyjah McLeod, Karma and Carol Phuntsok, Isabel Losada, Namgyal Tahkla, Owen Rigby, Tenzin Choegyal, Maureen Fallon, Frances Lamont, Carolyn Kennedy and many others for their support and encouragement.

For their blessings and their teachings, thank you to Karma Rinpoche, Dzongsar Khyentse Rinpoche, the Gyuto Monks, Sogyal Rinpoche, and His Holiness the Dalai Lama.

When I finished my first book, LEAVING NEVERLAND, my last excuse for not writing this as a novel disappeared.

I have great admiration for the Tibetan people and the Dalai Lama. I am a student of the Dharma and if there is a rank below novice that would be me. Any Dharmic mistakes are mine and will no doubt be dealt with karmically.

To my wife, Beth, my son Samuel, and my daughter, Aelysha; you keep my heart full. Without your love and support this book would not have been possible.

Thank you for reading this.

Tashi Delek,
Daniel Prokop